THE VALLEY ON THE
MOUNTAIN

Clinton Terwilliger

ISBN 979-8-88616-037-6 (paperback)
ISBN 979-8-88616-038-3 (digital)

Christian Faith Publishing
832 Park Avenue
Meadville, PA 16335
www.christianfaithpublishing.com

Printed in the United States of America

CONTENTS

PREFACE

Throughout this work, I have tried to convey a story that came to me as a set of dreams. I do not know nor understand the whole of it. A dream that happens in sequence over five nights is unusual but is exactly what happened and led to the writing of this story. When I shared the basics of this dream sequence with family members, they encouraged me to write it down as a memory to those future generations that would be interested in hearing this story.

Many of the stories in this work are based on true happenings. In the first part of the story, I mention a junkyard that we stopped at on one of our hunting trips to Alaska. It is true that I met a man with the same name as me. In real life, that is the extent of our interaction. However, his memory came to me in this dream, and the adventures told with him are fictional.

There are many who helped in the creation of this book. To my wife, Orleta, my deepest thanks both professionally and personally. The many hundreds of hours typing and retyping in attempts to get it right are commendable.

To my granddaughter Amber Gerard, who has been more than a supporter and advisor. To her, along with my wife, I owe a special debt of gratitude and appreciation. Her patience and judgment were indispensable. Without them, this book would not have been completed.

Probably every story, be it imaginary or a real desire of the heart, starts with a dream. As a young boy born and raised in the Nebraska Sandhills, I envisioned that when I grew up, I would go to Alaska, be a mountain man, wander aimlessly through the vast wilderness like some wide-eyed child, enjoying the savageness and excitement of living in the untamed wild. I would fish, hunt, and trap for a livelihood. I would build a log house, become a big game guide, kill the biggest moose ever, catch a fish so big that I wouldn't need to lie about it—just live a life of freedom in the wilderness. Instead, I got married, had four kids, and went to work as a welder-mechanic for a large timber company. Many obligations, many responsibilities, many bills, and I was hogtied for life.

Another dream, a real nighttime dream, came to me. The thing that made this dream different from others was that this dream was in sequence—five nights in a row, a different sequence to the same dream. This story is based on that set of dreams and a lot of imagination and fantasies.

There's another side to me too. I am a born-again Christian, and I know from the Word of God, the Bible, he has promised to never leave nor forsake me. That promise has been the main anchor of my life. Just like with Abraham, he is Jehovah Jireh, my complete source and resource. I read where it says in the word, *I have not seen the righteous forsaken nor his seed begging bread, but my God shall supply all of your need according to his riches in glory by Christ Jesus.*[1] That's a better guarantee than Good Housekeeping can offer. He is Alpha and Omega, the beginning and the end. He has the first and last say. I determined early in life to separate my life unto him and trust him for everything in every situation. He is omnipresent, everywhere all at once all the time. He is omnipotent; he can do all things; nothing is impossible for him. He is omniscient; he knows all things that all people will go through and knows it forever; he knows even your thoughts before you think them. This, then, is an allegory of the Christian life.

---

[1] Psalm 37:25, Philippians 4:19 (KJV).

GENESIS

Everything has a beginning—that is, everything but God.

My longtime friend and hunting partner Jim called one day and asked if I would like to go hunting in Alaska. Would I *what?* We left in early August and drove straight through to Tok, the first town in Alaska we came to on the ALCAN Highway. It took us forty-two hours.

We stopped on the outskirts of Tok at a sort of junk parts place to ask where we might get hunting licenses and tags. I met the owner, a man named James, at the doorway of a shed that had bear traps in the set position all over the walls and ceiling. I noticed across the way a little opposed-cylinder diesel engine chugging away to produce his electricity. I asked him, "How long have you had that?"

He said, "It has run forty-two years nonstop, only shutting it off to change oil. What are your names, and where are you from?"

"Well, this is Jim D., and I'm Clint Terwilliger, and we are from Chehalis, Washington," I said.

A fellow had come up and was sort of listening to our conversation and asked, "What did you say your last name is?"

I said "Well, it's Terwilliger."

"Would you spell it for me?" he asked.

"T-E-R-W-I-L-L-I-G-E-R," I said.

So he sticks out his hand and says, "Terwilliger, meet Terwilliger. I'm Freedom Terwilliger, born and raised in Chicken, Alaska, a town north of here. I want to talk with you, can we get together?"

I said, "Sure, I would like that also, but right now, I'm going hunting." I gave him my card. "I'll be home in about two weeks." I took down his number, we shook hands, and I left.

1

When I got home, my wife said some guy named Fred called, and I called him back. Long story short, he wanted to come down and see me right away. I invited him to come stay with me. I had a five-bedroom home. He accepted, and I picked him up at the Seattle Airport two days later.

He came into my home and was introduced to my family. He was one of those matter-of-fact type of people. I could tell just from the way he acted that he liked us right from the get-go. He asked a lot of questions, like "Where was I born?" "Who were my parents and their backgrounds?" "What were my likes and dislikes?" and so forth. I related that I like to hunt fish and trap. I just like to be in the great outdoors.

I had a little greenhouse operation going, and I showed him through that. So we were standing there in the greenhouse, and he says, "I'm seventy-seven years old and have no living relatives. Do you suppose we are related back somewhere?"

I told him my stepnephew had done a lot of family history research and said all Terwilligers have a common ancestor. He had come from Holland in 1663 with the first Dutch consignment on a ship called *De Arent* (the Eagle). His name was Everet Dirkson. At that time, it was customary for each succeeding generation to incorporate the first name into the last so Everet Dirkson's son was named Jan (pronounced John) Everetson. When the English retook New York, they made everybody take a common surname so John Everetson took the name Van Der Willigen, which, translated, means "place by the willows." Fred could trace his origin back to John Van Der Willigen. The next generation shortened it to Terwilliger, and all the Terwilligers, Tarwilligers, and some other spellings are from that same family. So we are related, and he was ecstatic.

I told him I had just finished building a log house, and of course, he had to see it. We were standing there in the log house, and he just blurted out, "Oh, you're the right one!"

"One what? One who?"

"You're the one I'm going to leave my money and all my Alaska land and holdings—you and your son after you. I want my legacy and the Terwilliger name to go on and on. Do you know a good, honest lawyer?" he asked.

"Mister, there ain't no such thing as a good, honest lawyer," I replied. "But I do know one who will treat us fair."

Long story short, he left us more than I could imagine. He told of a place several hundred miles north and west of Anchorage, a lake six miles long that he owned and all the property around it. It comprised some four thousand acres of land. It had a runway two miles long; he owned two Beaver airplanes. He had built a log home on it and had started a lodge and recreation area.

He also had some sixteen thousand acres he had purchased from his wife's people; she had been a native Alaskan of Indian descent. He had also said he had about ninety million dollars in the bank.

It all sounded like a fairy tale of sorts, and I sort of got the feeling maybe he was a little wacky, but the story all panned out as a lawyer dug into it. The paperwork was all in place; all we had to do now was occupy the land. I was heir to his fortune, most of it acquired by mining ventures. He was going home in two days.

As we sat having coffee, he confided in me. He said, "Nothing shakes you. Why?"

Well, there it was, the opportunity I had prayerfully waited for. I told him of my faith in Christ and his keeping power. He wanted to know more, so I related to him how Adam's sin had cost mankind his eternal life and all that had been restored by the shed blood, the death, the burial, and the resurrection of Christ. I told him that the soul has a body, and even though this body dies, God will give us a new one if we accept the Lord Jesus.

He began to sob hysterically and fell down on his knees and cried out to God to forgive him. He got up, seated himself, and began to speak in a language that could have only come down from the throne of God.

About an hour later, he regained himself, and these are his next words: "I am a new creature. I can die now without fear."

The next day, I took him back to the airport. It was the beginning of a new chapter in his life.

THE PLAN

He called me several times, almost weekly, relating his work, how he started big plans for a large expansion and a retreat center for Christian people, a mostly year-round place where people could experience the wild backcountry. He had plans for up to two hundred people per week, as well as a hunting and fishing guide service—all big plans, all fit into my dreams.

He spent the next summer building more lodge facilities, a design to heat the whole thing from a large hot spring just up the hill back of the lodge. More and more, the plan was for me to come up there and eventually ramrod the whole place for him. I would meet him at the airport in Anchorage, and my son Tony would come later after he graduated high school.

Fred had chartered a cargo plane to carry a load of supplies and necessities to build five outpost lodges on five different lakes on his extended property. As I understood it, the extended sixteen thousand acres was some thirty-five miles north of his home lodge property. We would have to build trails through what he described as "very brushy country."

He wanted lodging for several people in each place. I was to ramrod one crew of twenty-two men, and he would run the other one and hopefully have it workable in five years or less. He told me he had had a lot of supplies flown in by chopper to each area he planned to build in. He had also established two orphanages for native and Eskimo children, one in Tok and one in Dillingham on the Nushagak River near Bristol Bay.

Many, many plans, but I began to see this new creature grow with a tremendous outreach. How could he provide for so much? But like he said, "Is my new Lord limited?"

THE CRASH

I left for Anchorage on May 12, 1985, at 1:00 a.m. to begin a new episode in life. My son would come in late June to help me, and learn to help ramrod by doing so. Unc (short for Uncle Fred) told me to bring along anything I liked or wanted. He also asked me to purchase the eight-kilowatt Pelton wheel and generator from the Peltek company and send it to an address in Anchorage.

I was still fairly young—forty-seven, to be exact—full of ideas and energy. I had lots of imaginations and desires about almost everything, so in my luggage, I had put together ten army duffel bags. I had brought along what I figured I may never need or use. I had two of them full of underclothes and socks; one clear full of shirts, T-shirts, and pants; then one full of reloading equipment, brass, powder, primers, and a press and die for each caliber. I had fishing equipment and all my favorite guns. I had my dad's uncle's old ten-gauge L. C. Smith shotgun, a twelve-gauge pump, .30–30 Winchester, .308 Savage, a .44 Magnum Ruger carbine, a .358 Browning lever action, a .338 Lapua Magnum with a 6.5 to twenty-four scope. So I had three bags of hunting and fishing stuff besides a .44 magnum Redhawk revolver, and a .22 Reuger automatic that I carried on me.

I had another bag full of bee equipment, a smoker, a small two-frame extractor, beeswax, a little flat stamper thing with two plates to make celled pieces to put in the frames, and a lot of hive pieces that were knocked down along with a packet of bees with a queen.

Then I had one clear full of trees and berry bushes, hoping I could get them to grow. I had five dwarf apple trees, two peach trees, two pears and two apricots, five blackberry and five raspberry starts, and some grafting equipment. The pack of bees had enough food and water for about ten days. In those days, the airlines didn't search you or go through your stuff. I had to pay for extra luggage, though, and I also had two carry-on suitcases full of Western books, a cassette player, and cassettes with gospel and Western music. I had one suitcase full of all kinds of heirloom vegetable seeds, even potato eyes with little more than skins. I had wheat seed, corn seed, and alfalfa seed. This took up almost half of one of my carry-ons.

I arrived in Anchorage at 6:00 a.m. on May 12, 1985. Unc was there to meet me. We took my stuff over and loaded it onto the back of the plane. It was an ex-military boxcar-looking thing with two tails that extended back from the wings that were even with the two four-prop engines. The thing reminded me of a train boxcar. It had a ramp let-down door across the back that could accommodate loading vehicles. I walked up this ramp and stored my belongings alongside five large dog cages. One had a one-year-old Rottweiler puppy; one had three chickens; one, three ducks; another had three turkeys; and one had two little white pigs.

Fred said, "We are not leaving for three hours, so let's go eat our last supper [jokingly] and go shopping."

We bought more clothes, shoes, shirts, pants, underwear, and rubber boots—six pairs of everything and six more for him. I told him I had already brought a lot of clothes, but he just said, "We need you to have Alaska clothes," so I just relented with "Well, okay."

We didn't know it until then, but we were both the same size, even with the footwear. We lifted off at 9:00 a.m. and flew due north and a little west. There was a fuel place way out in the middle of nowhere. Unc had made arrangements to refuel there and then empty the bulk of it into tanks he had at the lodge. That plane was packed with what all, I didn't know. Fred rode in the front with the pilot, and I rode in the back with the birds and bees, the animals and trees.

The pilot had shown me how to pull the door up and lock it from inside. There was a little jump seat against the side wall and a seat belt of sorts that hung from some rings on the side wall and a little eight-inch window. There were several of these jump seats with little windows and a net bag next to each. I guess they still haul people sometimes; these jump seats folded up against the wall out of the way.

Two hours and forty minutes later, we landed to pick up the fuel. It took only about twenty minutes. Unc had a pair of walk-ie-talkie radios, of which I had one. He called to see if I wanted to get out and stretch. I told him no and that I was fine. Actually I had put on a lot of clothes and crawled into my minus-forty sleeping bag to stay warm.

The engines started, and we taxied down to the end of the run-way. He sat there awhile, and I moved so I could look out my lit-tle window. There was a lot of black smoke coming from the port engine. I got Unc on the radio and asked if anything was wrong. He said, "No, just a carburetor flooding. It will clear up soon," and it did. We took off and headed south west.

About twenty minutes later, I could feel the plane circling down and to port. I was cramped for space. There were forty-four thirty-six-wide, six-inch-thick, seven-foot-long foam rubber mattresses stacked up in front of me, and I was propped up against them, between them, and the ramp door. I had let Chance the Rottweiler out, and he was pushing against me and whining.

I could hear the engine running really rough. A voice came on the radio and said, "Prepare to crash, Clint. If I don't make it, I'll see you over yonder. Good luck and God bless."

Those were the last words I would ever hear from him. We seemed to have leveled off and straightened out. Then I could hear what I would later realize were willow branches and brush hitting the bottom of the plane, then we plowed onto a frozen lake with eight feet of snow on it. We had gone through three or four hundred yards of willow tops and now, two hundred yards of plowing through snow. I felt another fairly hard jolt, and the plane bounced and went slightly airborne and then nosedived, and I didn't know anything more for two days.

I heard what I thought was a slapping noise. Finally, I got awake enough to realize it was Chance licking my face. I had on two caps, a thick wool skullcap and another with flaps that fastened together on top or down under my chin. I got the top one off. Chance was trying to lick my bloody head and whine at the same time. It was pitch-black out. I was terribly thirsty, and I had a hard time getting my saliva working. My mouth was so dry. I decided to sit up, and my head started whirling, and I passed out again.

When I woke up, there was light from two small windows on either side. My radio was on the padding next to me. I tried to call out, but there was no answer. The ducks were hissing, the chickens cackling, the turkeys chirping, the pigs grunting, and I was saying over and over, "Oh, God. Oh, God."

I got out of the bag and stood up. I found water bottles in the net bag next to the jump seat. I drank and gave water to the birds and animals. I gave thanks to God, and then it hit me I didn't know who I was. I knew I had been in a plane crash, but who am I?

THE FIRST TWENTY DAYS

Day 1

I could remember I had left on the twelfth of May, but how long
had I been out? The plane was on its nose in a pile of small logs,
mostly four to six inches in diameter. The back of the plane was
at a thirty-five-degree angle above me. No door, no way out from
back here, except by a let-down cargo door.

Things had crunched forward a bit. I wanted to get to the front,
so I started pulling out the large metal trunks loaded with God-
knows-what all. The first one I opened was a snack food tote—lots
of candy bars and granola bars, drinks in little boxes with a straw
in the side. I stopped right there and ate four granola bars and gave
four to the birds and four to the animals and some jerky to Chance
and ate some myself. I got the bees out and put some water in a little
thing provided.

It was getting dark. I prayed most of the night. Surely, God
would send somebody to find me. That was my prayer. I hoped it
was also God's will.

Day 2

I was up as soon as it got light enough to see. The days were still
short, and it was bitter cold, at least compared to what I was used
to. I realized my skullcap was glued to my head by the dried blood. I
got some water on it, wetted the wool skullcap, and finally got it off.
There was new bleeding. I got out a new T-shirt and tore it up and
made a bandage out of it after I water sterilized the wound.

I rested a bit and went to work on the large metal trunks that were stored down the one side. I pulled them up to the other back-side with a cable come-along that I had found in one of the containers. It had a variety of tools in it. I was cramped for room, and it was very awkward, so I decided to try and get the ramp cargo door open and try to figure out some way to unload a lot of this stuff.

I couldn't quite reach the area I needed by standing on one of the trunks that was on the mattresses, and they wobbled every which way, so I climbed up on the slats of wood on the wall that were meant for tie-downs. I got the cam-over-type lock downs loose and in the open position. I got the brake released and the ratchet cranks that turned a pipe that went clear across the plane top. It had cables on it that were attached to either side of the ramp door.

As they unwound, it let the door down. By the reverse process, it pulled the door up and shut. The top of the ramp door was slightly past the center of straight up and down because of the tipped-up angle of the plane. I got hold of a slat on the top edge, pulled myself up, and using my other hand, pushed hard on the top of the ramp door. It came back past the center, and the cranks or brakes weren't fixed right, and so the door just fell open until it hit the end of the cable. That jar was enough to jolt the plane, and it fell down into a nearly level position.

I fell on the floor area but didn't appear to break anything. My head hurt, my shoulder hurt, my ribs hurt. I just lay there and fell asleep. When I woke up I was shivering and very cold. I found my sleeping bag and crawled in and slept until it got light outside.

Day 3

It was cold, and the wind was blowing. My beard and mustache had frost in them. The plane was level about ten feet above what appeared to be a creek bed. I cranked the cargo door back to level with the plane floor. The two tails of the plane were back about another fifteen feet and above a large windswept flat rock area.

There was a gap of about four feet or so between the outer edge of the cargo door and the edge of the flat rock. Now I had to get across that gap. I was too stiff and sore to try to jump across. I might fall, and that could be my end. I started pushing crates around and opened some to see what was in them. These were handcrafted trunks of diamond plate aluminum with a watertight lid that had a rubber gasket all around the inside of the lid.

There were also several wooden crates. I found two with power saws in them. One was a Stihl 066 with a large long bar, a midsize one with a twenty-inch bar, and a small lightweight one with a fourteen-inch bar. There were fuel cans, chain oil, wrenches, files, extra chain, repair parts, and a repair manual for each.

I didn't see a ladder or the end of one, so I assumed there wasn't one. There was a large spool of what is referred to as "fish tape" that can be air blown through a tube to attach wiring for telephone wire to pull it through the tube. It was on a four-foot round aluminum spool. I estimated that there could be fifteen or twenty miles of the stuff on that one spool. The stuff is extremely strong, 1,600 pounds breaking strength, and it's only about five sixteenth of an inchwide and maybe one sixteenth of an inch thick.

I braided some together with cross pieces to form a ladder and attached it to the roof area of the plane at the top edge above the cargo door then over and down into the creek bed. I let down the midsize power saw with fuel and needed tools. I found some six-inch-diameter poles. I cut several of these about seven foot long and bound four together with a two-inch-wide, twenty-four-inch-long piece of round stock. I tied a piece of my fish tape rope to one end of a short stick and the other end facing it toward the plane gap and pitched that end piece over into the back of the plane. I reclimbed up my rope ladder and pull lifted my crossover bridge onto the end of my cargo door. Now I can walk over on my approximately two-foot-wide bridge.

There was a part of the flat rock area that had a natural ramp about twelve foot wide that went over into the creek bed. It was slightly downhill, but the creek bed was so steep that it connected at the creek level about thirty feet upstream. It looked almost level but was about a five-foot descent to the right side of the creek bed.

Out in front of where the nose of the plane was an area about three acres in size that was covered over with trees, some twelve to twenty foot deep in logs, some as much as twelve inches in diameter, but most were from four to six inches in diameter. I found out later that the creek that fed this came down from the north at a very steep angle, hit a rock wall, turned at a right angle along that wall, and shot out into that three-acre basin. Then in the spring runoff, it piled these logs and debris up to as much as twenty foot high. At low-normal flow, the water hit the rock wall, turned right for about twenty feet, then left around the wall end and down approximately 110 feet underneath the plane and out into the lake that started about fifty feet behind the back of the plane.

Another day was spent, and so was I. I had found a crate of cots that had to be set up, so I set one up in the back of the plane and put a foam rubber mattress on it along with my minus-forty-degree sleeping bag. I ate a couple of granola bars and some jerky, crawled into bed, and fell asleep.

Day 4

Another cold morning. Between being cold and my sore body, it was hard to crawl out of bed. I had slept in my clothes, except for my shoes, so I got up; put on my shoes, coat, and a hat; then faced another day. The sun came up, it warmed up, and I started unloading more cargo.

I cleaned off an area on the flat rock next to the left side that had a rock overhang. I cleaned the snow off an area maybe twenty by thirty feet. I had pulled several of the lighter trunks over and carried them off and opened them to see what was in them. There was a small, quarter-size metal piece pop riveted to the cover of each trunk with a number on it. Inside was a list of what was in that box and another that listed how many and how much of each. This one held snacks: candy bars, granola bars, chips, cookies, jerky—anything you could just grab and eat along the way with the little boxes of juice drinks that you simply punched a little provided straw into and drink.

Day 5

I unloaded about five dozen five-gallon buckets that were slid together and a pack of lids for the lot. I took two of these at a time, unpacked stuff into them, carried them over, and put them all back into the now-empty trunk. These trunks were two feet by two feet by three feet long, about twelve square feet or ninety gallons if filled with liquid. I got twenty-eight trunks off that day, along with forty-three mattresses. I put several mattresses over and around the food boxes to keep out the cold.

Day 6

I was working first light till dark. The days were getting longer, and my head still hurt. I would have dizzy spells, and I would forget what I was doing or where I was at. This usually lasted less than a minute or two. I figured out I had a cut about two inches long. I could lay my little finger in it. I had no way to sew it up, so I just would keep the hair pulled out and back and let it fill in as it healed. I would have that scar for life.

My right shoulder and rib cage next to my backbone hurt all the time. There was a wide bump in that area. I was pretty sure there were broken ribs or a pulled muscle or ligament. If I moved just wrong, I would hear and feel a little popping noise, but that really didn't hurt when it happened.

Every day, it got a little better, but I did most of my work with my left hand or arm. Evidently, when the plane hit and flipped up on its nose, I had probably slammed up against the mattresses and then was catapulted upward and hit the ceiling area. I had some huge bruises, the worst one from my right knee to my thigh. That area was a little sore, but my shoulder and ribs were the worst.

Day 7

I spent another day digging out and taking inventory. I hit the jackpot! There was an RTV with a dump bed and a five-thousand-pound high cable capacity winch on the front. It also had a four-by-five-foot bed with fold-up side panels. In the bed were ninety cases of twelve each wide-mouth pint canning jars with enough extra lids to be able to use each jar twelve times. Would I need these?

Then surprise number 2 revealed itself! I dug a little farther and found a 4×4 ATV, two pull-behind self-dump trailers, four fifteen-foot-long canoes, a twelve-foot skiff, two nine-horse outboard motors, eight wheelbarrows, four with one wheel in front and four with two wheels. The wheels were aluminum, and the tires looked like the tube-tire type, but they had a dense rubber core that would never go flat. They were about sixteen inches in diameter. There was a sixteen-foot orchard ladder and a step ladder that could be extended out or folded up to make a regular step ladder. There were fourteen ten-inch round aluminum pipes, three-eighth-inch-thick walls twenty-two feet long. They had an expanded end, so the end of the next pipe could slide inside with a rubber O ring and a cam-over type lock on two sides.

Inside of these were ten eight-inch of the same nomenclature, then ten six, then ten four, and then ten one-and-a-half-inch pipes, and the other four ten-inch had eighteen each of the one and a half inch, so I had 1,780 feet of one and a half inch, two hundred feet each of eight, six and four. There were four crates of end-fitting valves and elbows of various degrees. There were four two-thousand-watt generators and four four-hundred-watt generators. The two-thousand ones had cords that would connect the two-thousand-watt generators together to supply four thousand watts.

There were four one-hundred-foot extension cords, two of which had light sockets every eight feet. Two twelve-volt chargers, eight six-volt batteries to tie two together to make twelve volts. Lots of ten-, twelve-, and fourteen-gauge wiring. There was a large roll of number 8 copper-insulated wire. I got it all off-loaded but the pipe, the ATV, the RTV, canoes, skiff, and fuel bladders. RTV means "rough-terrain vehicle," and ATV means "all-terrain vehicle."

There were four oblong, round wood stoves that had a flat top with a stainless steel water heater with a curved side to fit the curvature of the stove. They had a grate so you also burn coal and five pieces of tapered fit-together stove pipe. There were four screw-on legs and a flat plate to extend the top surface. All the extras were stored inside the stove itself.

In a separate pack, there were twenty pieces of six-inch galvanized stove pipe that were extra thick and long-lasting.

Day 8

I needed a wider crossover from the cargo ramp to the flat rock area, so I made another two-foot-wide bridge part and spacer to hold them the right distance apart and braced under and down to the creek bed. I got the ATV, RTV, pipe, and everything but the fuel bladders and stuff I used to live aboard off. The skiff had a small two-wheel trailer. I took the skiff off and used the trailer to off-load the pipe. Now I could see into the cabin through a small window in the bulkhead door. The door was bent and locked, making it unopenable.

I shined a light through the window. The pilot's body was two thirds the way out the front window; his seatbelt was off. I think he must have lived long enough to crawl out the broken window. The passenger was missing his head. There was an eight-inch piece of log going through the cabin and out through the side, so it must have taken off that person's head. The bodies were frozen, so there was no smell. I hoped those men, whoever they were, knew the Lord.

Day 9

I brought one of the stoves back in close to the back of the plane. I broke out the farthest back little window and got a chimney out. I built a fire and filled the water heater with snow. I kept filling it with snow until I had it clear full of hot water. It had a little spigot on the front to get the water out of it. Four of the one-hundred-gallon fuel bladders were gas; four were diesel. Each had a little hand pump in an attached fabric bag. They were military surplus as well.

There was a brand-new leather couch and a recliner chair that I had left aboard. I got one of the heavy floor mats from one of the tents and used it for a rug of sorts for the floor of the plane. I had found several tarps of various sizes and hung one over the cargo door opening. I had the fish tape spool on its side for a table and a folding chair. There were forty-four folding chairs, forty-four cots, and forty-four sleeping bags. Now I had a dry, warm place to live.

Day 10

Plenty of unfinished work. I took two of the trunks and put the contents into several other trunks. I stacked them on top of each other and used them for a cupboard of sorts. I filled the cupboard with some paper plates, pots, pans, food, and coffee (the things I wanted handy when I needed them). There was no coffee pot that I had found yet, but maybe there would be in some of the crates or trunks that I had yet to open. For now, I would just boil it in a pan.

Day 11

I would open more crates and trunks and take more inventory today. I dragged out crates where I had them stored under the overhang. I would erect one or two of the large tents so I could get the supplies under some sort of cover. I opened one eight-foot-long crate to find a bunch of one-inch aluminum pipes that had little aluminum square fins about one inch apart the full length with little neoprene connector things on each end. The fins made the pipe square and four inches across. They were a part of a radiator hot water heater. I found the top and bottom manifolds in another crate. Altogether, there was enough for three, eight by ten foot heaters. Everything was ready to use. I would just have to fit it all together according to the instructions in the pamphlet provided.

Another crate had two small Mantis tillers. They amounted to a power hoe of sorts to cultivate with. Another had a large Troy-Bilt walk-behind tiller. I opened about twenty of the trunks, as I now call them. Many of these contained food. I found one more that was marked "snacks," three that had dried apples, pears, and other assorted fruits. Another had all kinds of nuts, mostly peanuts, cashews, and smokehouse almonds. One crate was full of bagged coffee, ninety-six five-pound bags to add to the ninety-six cans I had previously discovered. Another crate had teas, both regular and herbal. There was twenty one-gallon-sized orange drink mix called Tang. Some other flavors included lemon and grapefruit. One was full of large cheeses wrapped in cheesecloth and dipped in a paraffin wax. One had all sorts of dried meats, salami, pepperoni, summer sausage, etc. One had towels, including some dish, bath, and washrags.

It also contained pot holders and a meat grinder that was hand operated and had attachments to stuff sausages with. There was a grain mill and two inverters to make twelve-volt batteries into 110 AC. One was a five-kilowatt inverter and one one-kilowatt inverter. There were four little high-speed blender things to grind coffee beans. They would only do enough to make one pot of coffee at a time.

The ninety-six bags I had found were all whole beans, so this was a great discovery! One trunk had canned butter, canned peanut butter, jelly, jam, and hundreds of packs of dried Milkman brand milk. One packet makes one quart of milk. There was baking powder, baking soda, and other baking supplies, even a cookbook! One had pancake flour, Bisquick, and crackers in separate tin containers. One was full of Hamburger Helper, various dried soups, dried onions and garlic, and a full line of spices in one- and two-pound bags.

One had four fifty-pound bags of a dry milk mix to start bummer orphan lambs on. It seems that one of the cooks was of Chinese descent and would only use this for cooking puddings and gravies. It is said this product makes a much smoother and tastier finished product.

There were several bags of salt, sugar, brown sugar, syrups, dry yeast, dry beef and chicken stock, ranch, and Russian dried dressing mix (just add water). Another two had sixteen slabs of cured bacon, sixteen hams, sixteen cured pork loins called Canadian bacon. One had all sorts of sweet rolls and so forth, all in Seal-a-Meal individually wrapped. There were cans of whole chicken, tuna, and smoked salmon. Two said, "Personal, Fred," and there was also a really big three-by-three-by-four-foot trunk made of diamond plate aluminum.

I just set these aside. I was shy about opening someone else's belongings even if they weren't around any longer. I still had enough of my wits that I surmised this might have belonged to the man in the cabin with the pilot. Was that a man named Fred, and who was I? I would try so hard to think. I would strain so hard that it would hurt to try to remember.

Day 12

This was actually fourteen days after the crash, but I still didn't know what day it was on the calendar that I had because I didn't know how long I had been unconscious, and I didn't know what the actual date was on the calendar. I knew, or thought, I had a watch that showed the day, but I couldn't find my watch. I didn't have a clock. I was good at calculating how much day was gone and how much remained by the sun, so for now, that was my timepiece. I have been here for nearly two weeks after I woke up—still no rescue.

Day 13

I got the two tents set up that I needed to house stuff in. They were heavy-duty with extra heavy canvas and a thick pipe or structures and heavy floor covering with a rubberized one side. I had one of those in the plane, and I put one in one of the tents that I had set up. I rolled and stashed the other two.

Oh, I prayed several times a day, always asking God to help me get rescued. I didn't know what a sovereign God had in mind for me, but I hoped it wasn't for me to stay here very long. I would say, "God, if I'm going to be here a long time, please tell me," but he was silent. I didn't understand that, and I still don't, but we sometimes just have to say God is God and trust. That's part of faith.

Last night, during the night, I felt a little lurch in the plane. I remembered again in the morning, so I got busy and cut some poles to brace up and stabilize the two tails. They were about twenty feet or so apart and with a tail brace between them. There were about eight feet above the flat rock area. I went down and under the plane just behind the back edge of the wings. One wing rested on the woodpile, the other on a huge rock outcrop. If we had been over to the left twenty feet, the plane nose would have dived right into that rock. I cut a twelve-foot-long-by-about-ten-inch-thick pole and used the power saw to shape it to the curvature of the belly of the plane. I got a pole to go upright under each end and one for the middle, got them pretty much in place, and then drove the bottoms over with a sledgehammer to tighten them in. I slept well that night.

Day 14

It's Friday. Oh well, I'm not superstitious anyway. It was, by my thinking, the twenty-eighth of May. My head was causing me to have goofy thoughts sometimes. I was learning to override it some, but I would sometimes see things that weren't there. I thought I saw a boat one time, and when I came out of my delusion just before I stepped aboard, I was standing right on the edge of the rock area. That next step would have put me over the ten-foot drop onto the ice.

I decided to do a little scouting trip. The snowdrifts were settling as it warms up a bit; they froze at night and formed a hard crust on top that would hold up the ATV for the most part. I hooked up one of the dumpcarts behind the ATV and rode around the south side of the lake. I figured it was more shallow there in case I fell through the ice.

I cut through the ice with the big power saw and got moss on the end of the blade, so I knew it was pretty shallow along here. There appeared to be a valley that led up and away from the west side. In order to leave what I have begun to call home, I rode across the far end of the flat top rock area, perhaps eighty feet wide at the widest place and 140 long. It had a natural ramp at the far end, went down from about thirty feet back, and was about ten feet wide at the bottom edge of the ice that would be water when it thawed. I took a shovel, a pickax, and a cob fork with my .358 Browning lever action rifle. I stayed close to the south side and west Side.

The northwest side had a high wall that went straight down into the water. It was deep, and there were little seeps in the wall where steam came out and evaporated. I was spooked to go over on that side even to walk.

I had gone up the west side valley maybe two hundred feet or so when I saw this tan-colored stuff. It looked odd, so I got off the quad, and I felt it. It was frozen but dry enough that it crumbled some. I chipped at it with the pickax. Soon, I realized it was sphagnum peat moss. I had found a peat bog! This was drier than on the valley floor. I took the power saw and cut out a chunk about two feet by two feet and strapped it on the back of the quad. I rode up more and picked my way to the rim of the canyon. I had to shovel snow twice, but I made it okay.

There was a vast open country before me surrounded and covered in white snow—so serene, so beautiful. There were some dark-looking low bluffs to my right and to the north and up a bit. When I got to the base of them, I found a lot of crumbly stuff that I realized was pumice stone. Most of this was fine granulated stuff about one eight of an inch in size. I dug around under the snow out a ways from the cliffside and found it was all pumice, thousands and thousands of square yards of it. I shoveled the cart two thirds full and went on.

There were windblown spots where there was no snow, and there was old low brush all over. I wasn't worried about getting lost. All I had to do was follow my tracks back. I saw what I thought at first was a wolf coming across the prairie toward me. I grabbed the .358 off my shoulder and stopped the quad. I have never killed a wolf before, but I was about to. He stopped out about 150 yards with just his head above the snowline. I put my scope on him and realized he was wagging his tail. Then I saw a part of a collar and realized it was Chance, who had followed me. "It was about your last day to live, Chancey boy," I said to myself. He was happy for a ride in the wagon.

We went on, and there was the end of a hill. As we went around where one side had been torn away, I saw a black chunk of stuff that had fallen off. I got off the quad and examined a piece of it. It appeared to be coal. I threw it down hard, and it didn't break. I stomped on it, and it still didn't break. I hit it with the side of the pickax, and it shattered that time. I was pretty sure it was coal. I picked up enough chunks to fill the rest of the trailer, the biggest pieces being some sixteen inches across. The cart was rounding up full, so I put Chance on my lap. I had to hold on to him, but he finally relaxed and settled down.

In the distance, I saw that the country dropped away, and I thought by the sun that it could be where I had come up out of the canyon. It was probably about two miles away. In about a mile or so, I crossed my old tracks and followed them back. I had saved myself at least ten miles. I was glad to get home; it was almost dark.

I fixed some mac and cheese, some dried fruit, coffee, and spam. I had a cinnamon roll for dessert. I built a fire and pulled up one of the folding chairs and said my prayers, counting my blessings. Praise God just because he is God and because I love him. I knew deep down that somehow, all this fit into his plans for me and felt content. Chance came over and lay down at my feet—a good day, a really wonderful day in fact. I have seen a vast, vast, open country-side. I have found peat moss, pumice, and coal. I put a big chunk on the fire just to see if it would burn. I crossed over *Jordan* (as I now called the dry creek bed) and crawled into my cot bed, prayed a bit, and fell asleep.

Day 15

I can tell that the days are getting longer. I took the quad and the cob fork, a tool about the size of a big scoop shovel with tines about one inch apart to get a big load of peat moss.

The next day, I took the RTV and a trailer. I could get about three yards per trip this way and after rechecking the ice, I cut straight across the middle then up the ramp to dump each load and went back for another. The RTV had a hydraulic dump. The dumpcart self-dumped by pulling a front hold-down lever, and it was overbalanced behind the axel and self-dumped. I made a trip every forty minutes and had forty yards out by dark.

Day 16

I worked more on gathering peat moss. I was able to haul another forty yards, along with four yards of coal.

Day 17

I went all the way to the pumice field. It was about twelve miles away. This stuff is light. I took the RTV, both trailers, and several gunnysacks. I had probably forty of them in a bale. I filled the RTV, on day 18. The two dumpcarts, and several sacks tied on top of each. I had close to twenty yards of pumice. Hard work, but I always felt good afterward, like I had accomplished something.

Day 19

I went on an excursion to the south of the lake. That is where the plane had come in through the willow tops. The moose had eaten the tops down to where they were about half an inch in diameter. They grow back thicker and thicker each year. The plane had skimmed through some three hundred yards of this and slowed the plane way down. Then we plowed onto the frozen lake through eight-foot-deep snow. Then we hit a small island about eighty feet from where the plane rested. This had popped the plane into the air momentarily, and it had hit and flipped onto its nose about fifty feet up and to one side of the creek bed.

There were a lot of moose droppings on top of the snow amongst the willows. Moose will produce about ten pounds of manure a day. That's three hundred pounds a month per animal. I was able to collect about ten yards of this. Rotting moose manure, like horse manure, will produce a lot of heat as it rots. It looks a lot like horse droppings, except it's more square. The ice was starting to look a little conky, so I decided to stay off it.

Day 20

By my figuring, it was the third of June—thereabouts. I sat by my evening campfire when the wind came up and started blowing pretty hard. It was a warm wind out of the south. I put my campfire out and built one in the stove on the plane. I pulled my canvas shutter across the back and went to bed.

I lay there, still awake, when I heard this roaring sound like ten freight trains. "What the…! Whatever is that?"

Then it hit me—lots of water! A gully washer, and it was coming right down this creek. I grabbed my clothes, sleeping bag, and gun and raced across Jordan. The water was roaring right under the plane about two feet below. I was sure it would take the plane; my fuel bags, my stove, the couch, and chair would all be gone, washed out into the lake, and when the ice was gone, so would the plane be, along with the pilot and that other guy. Why hadn't I taken the time to get them out and bury them? God forgive me.

Well, I figured out what probably happened was that somewhere upstream, the trees, wood, and debris must have formed a temporary dam. When it broke, all that water came rushing down. The rain was still coming, the wind still blowing, but the water was going down. It rained hard for the next three days. I slept in one of the tents, the one with the stove and floor mat. The ice had broken up and washed away. The plane was still there, so I moved back in.

I needed to try to make a greenhouse and get some garden stuff planted. I had all the makings for soil but no lime to get the PH down in the peat moss. Peat moss has quite a bit of tannic acid in it and makes it more acidic. I had noticed when I was scouting the south side willows that there was something shiny off to the southwest corner. I decided to go see what it was. I got out one of the canoes and paddled over to that corner.

In a little flat open area, there were three big aluminum watertight containers made of the same diamond plate, only thicker. They each were eight feet wide, eight feet high, and twelve foot long. They were jam-packed full. They must have come in by chopper and then made more trips to fill them. They each had a four-by-seven-foot door, with a rubber gasket to seal out the moisture. There were more materials to build lodges with, more fuel bladders, and bags and bags of cement. There was also lime to mix with cement and sand and some bags of aluminum powder.

I remembered then that I had told that man, whom had come down to Chehalis to visit me, about a formula to make chinking to go between the logs in log houses. The formula is two parts sand, two parts cement, two parts lime, and a teaspoon of aluminum powder to make a five-gallon bucket of chinking mix. The powder oxidizes when wet and makes bubbles in the chinking that cause it to swell as it dries and makes an airtight fit. I found a band saw mill, which would have to be put together.

There were ten boxes each of ten blades and a sharpener also that would have to be set up. Lots of power tools: a hand planer, a handheld power hacksaw, a table saw, a three-tiered thing with a cast metal housing, and a five-horse electric motor. It also had a ten-horse gas engine. I could find no nomenclature manual.

There was a rotary hammer with drill bits for wood and metal or star drills to drill rock, a gold screed to separate gold from sand, four more power saws, two long aluminum carts about ten feet long with three axles each, a one-eighth-inch-thick four-by-eight sheet of steel, and another four-by-eight that was one quarter inch thick. There were lots of rebar in several sizes, hand tools, hammers, sledge-hammers, splitting mauls, wedges, lots of copper wire, five hundred more feet each of four-inch and six-inch pipes in ten-foot lengths, garden hoses, a hand scythe, a hedge trimmer with a four-foot-long blade, and a lot of stuff I never figured I would use.

There were boxes and boxes of different sizes and lengths of screws, several screw guns, hammer screw guns, boxes and boxes of bolts and lag screws, regular bolts in various lengths and sizes. There was at least a thousand gallons of diesel fuel in those rubber fuel bladders, more cable winches and chain falls, one huge twenty-ton chain fall. I thought to myself, *Now why would I ever need that?*

There was a smaller band saw that was upright. There were twenty lengths of half-inch stainless pipe ten feet long with threaded ends, a roll of one-quarter-inch stainless cable, and another roll of galvanized. Each roll was five thousand feet long. Lots of rope and four full boxes of dynamite, and that was just what I could see from the doorway. God only knows what else there would be. I took five bags of lime back to the canoe, shut the doors back up, and went back to my dwelling place. Later on, I would try to unload and move around enough stuff to try to get a complete inventory.

As I started back in the canoe, there was a large moose calf at the lakeside, drinking. Oh boy, fresh meat, not just for me but for the animals and birds. I kept everything, even the guts. I can feed them to the chickens, pigs, and turkeys. I stretched out the skin on some poles, scraped off the fat, knocked the head open, and got the brains out—no, not to eat. There is enough tannic acid in any animal's brain to tan its hide. I suppose God had it all figured out that way. You have to cook the brain and make it into a slurry, then paint it onto lightly dried skin, let that cure for about a week to ten days, then work the skin back and forth over a pole end until it is supple and pliable.

After three trips, I had the moose all packed back over, cut up, and stored in Ziploc bags and against the still-frozen rock wall with some mattresses on it to keep it insulated. I had saved the testicles. I cut the outer membrane off, cut each in half, pounded them out into four small patties, breaded them with the egg and cracker crumbs, fried them up, and had Nebraska-style mountain oysters. I was raised on these from my childhood, and it seemed the natural thing to do. They taste like real oysters, so don't knock it till you try it.

I got back to gardening. I put down a layer of peat, then a layer of creek sand, a thin layer of pumice, some moose manure for fertilizer, some lime for sweetener, then some more of each until I had a base that was about eighteen inches deep. Then I plowed it back and forth with the ATV blade until it was well mixed. I piled some four-inch-long logs along the back wall about three feet out and sixteen inches deep. The soil inside would support that side, and I propped large rocks against the outside, then I planted my potatoes across the back, a double row about eighty feet long. I also had an open area of soil about eighteen inches deep. I planted my heirloom seeds, carrots, cabbage, cauliflower, broccoli, rutabagas, turnips, onions, peppers (both sweet and hot), and many others. My horseradish roots and asparagus roots too. Heirloom seed comes back the same as the original plant. You can save the seed from year to year. Hybrid seed will grow back a bunch of stuff of different varieties of whatever was used to hybridize it, and you don't know what you'll get, if anything at all.

I got busy building my greenhouse. There was a wall behind the flat area that was about one hundred feet high, but there was an overhang on the bottom that was about twelve or fifteen feet and twenty-two feet high on the top outer edge. I had found several rolls of six-mil clear plastic, thirty-two feet wide by 150 long. I cut thirty thirty-foot-long poles four inches in diameter on the bottom and about two on the top. I got the rotary hammer out and hooked up two of the two-thousand-watt generators to run it. I strung out a power cord so I wouldn't have to move the generators too much. I drilled half-inch holes in a straight line in the rock about thirty-two feet out from the back wall. I cut half-inch rebar into short pieces to drop in the holes after I wedged the top end of the thirty-foot poles just under the lip of the overhang, then a piece of rebar in the hole at the bottom to hold it in place. I took some three-inch poles and split them in half endways for a piece across the top to nail the plastic to.

If you split a pole from the center, it will split out straight. If you split it from one end to another, it will taper down to one end. I split out more pieces to go across the bottom and split out some one-inch-thick lathe to screw over the top and bottom with the plastic sandwiched between to hold it in place. I used screws so I could get it apart easier when I took it off in the fall.

When I finished, I had a greenhouse about thirty-two feet wide, one hundred feet long. It got too hot many days, and I would open the ends to let it cool. I was amazed I had all this know-how and still didn't know who I was. It really bugged me. I could sense the presence of God in my life; his Spirit would bear witness with my spirit. I would speak with the Spirit, and I would speak with the understanding also. I knew just about anything, but I didn't know who I was or who the two guys were who had died.

Every few days, my mind would slip, and I would hallucinate or become confused, sometimes for several hours at a time. I realized it was because of the head wound. Sometimes if I caught it as soon as I felt myself slipping, I could partly override it. I knew life has its crashes, but this one had really destroyed me. It had divorced me from the ones I loved, and I was mentally disoriented because of it.

FACING THE GIANT

I pulled back the curtain that I used to cover the back of the plane. I pulled my recliner chair around, facing the back of the flat rock area. I was having coffee and a roll and admiring all the hard work, feeling the sun on my face, watching the fish rise on the lake, swatting mosquitoes. They would land on me but not bite me. How lovely this place, just the sort of place I had dreamed of, even prayed for. "Be careful what you pray for," someone had once said to me.

Now all I wanted was to be rescued. It was so lonely here. I could have easily thought of it as a wasteland, a howling wilderness, but the sheer beauty of it caused a deep and profound joy in me. Chance was on the flat top. I had the .358 lying by the recliner side. I was going to clean it pretty soon. I heard Chance start to growl and then whine. A giant grizzly was going toward him on his back legs and popping his jaws at Chance. I said, "Mr. Giant Philistine, don't you know that I'm under a covenant with God, and you're not?"

He just pivoted around and came toward me, all the time popping off his mouth. Well, I reached down, picked up the .358, put the crosshairs under his chin, said a short prayer, and dropped the hammer. He, who later turned out to be a she, never knew what hit her. Oh no! She had two yearling cubs with her. One came back past me and headed up the creek. I snapped a shot at him, rolled him; he got up bawling and running up the creek. The other one went toward the far end past the greenhouse, and I never knew where he went.

I followed the one that went up the steep creek bed. This part of the creek bed went about thirty feet past the ramp with an incline that went up at about a forty-degree angle for thirty more feet then leveled out. So there was a flat area sticking out along the wall about

27

fourteen feet wide and fifty or so feet long that ended where a part of the wall went to the left. The creek water shot out behind this part of the wall then turned back left and on down under the plane and out into the lake.

There was a large area where, at high water, this creek would wash trees and brush and debris out in a three-acre flat that was from there clear down to the front of the plane. I have mentioned this before, but I wanted to show where this spot was located. The right wing of the plane rested on the other end of this debris field.

When I got to the end of this little flat area where the wall cut me off, there was a place about four or five feet wide that went back into the main wall on my right. I could hear the bear crying back in there. I stood there with the .358 ready when Chance came up and started growling and barking. The noise from the bear stopped. I waited a few minutes, then went sort of up and in, pulled some brush out of the way, and could see the back part of the bear. I got ahold of his back leg and pulled him out. He was already really fat. I turned him onto his back and rolled the guts out of him, lots of nice white fat that I could cook with or whatever I might need it for.

I looked back in the place I had pulled him out of, and it looked like there was an opening at the top that went farther in. I would have to climb farther up in the end to see into that hole, so I let it go for now. About fifteen or twenty feet to the right was another similar-looking inverted area in the wall. I had planned to build a chicken coop today and try to get the bees content. I had made a hive and got them to accept it, but I had to feed them sugar to survive. That was all off for now.

I gutted and quartered the mama bear, hung the meat, and got the hide laid out and the fat scraped off. Then I heard whining over next to the wall. I pulled the plastic back, and there was a very small baby bear, so mama bear had two older cubs still with her as well as this little guy. Now I had an orphan on my hands.

I didn't have the heart to just kill the innocent little guy. He was so cute. There is really no such thing as an ugly baby. Even baboons are so ugly and yet so cute. I got the bummer lamb milk mix out and mixed it in some warm water. I cut the little finger off a rubber glove and cut a small slit in the end then stretched it over a plastic water bottle. Well, I got some warm milk into that little guy. He drank about a third of the bottle.

I had to get up every two hours at night after that and feed him. He was a he, so I named him Samson, but he became known to me as just *Bear*. Chance was jealous at first, but he got over it, and they became friends and spent a lot of time playing together. I finished tanning the bearskins and made rugs out of them. The yearling, I laid over the back of my couch.

INVESTIGATING MY FUTURE

I built a twelve-by-twelve-by-six-foot-high bird pen. I turned the ducks loose on the lake. I had a whole duffel bag full of precut boards to make beehives out of. I put some together with a pre-made cell plate of beeswax to get them started. Whoever had put this cargo together had just about covered all the bases. There was a pallet of cracked corn and one pallet of dog food. I had to break it down to unload it, but there were other crates that I had simply pulled off and stored them for now.

I still had to get the fuel bladders off. They weighed some eight hundred or so pounds each. If I just pull them off with the RTV, I might tear a hole in it, so I would have to figure something out later. I was building a backlog of work, so I tried to prioritize and work long hours to try to catch up. Samson and Chance were always under foot, but I enjoyed their company.

I took time to go up and investigate that hole in the wall. There were three of us, so I nicknamed us the "Hole in the Wall Gang." I took the pick and shovel and always the .358. It was a Browning lightweight short barrel and could be handled with one hand if need be. A .358 is simply a .308 necked up to a .35 caliber. I handloaded fifty-three grains of 3031 IMR rifle powder with a 180-grain flat nose bullet. It had a lot of knockdown but wasn't really adequate for a charging grizzly or mad bull moose. I liked it because it was light-weight and could be used quickly if need be.

I had brought all my reloading equipment, which included eighty pounds of 3031 powder, eighty-five pounds of 4350 powder, and twenty pounds of H1000 powder. I figured I had enough to reload about twenty thousand rounds. It was overkill to say the least, no pun intended.

I had a pretty good flashlight that was in one of the screw gun kits. I shined a light up into that hole. I crawled up, and in about ten feet, I could get my head up enough to see a larger room behind a blockage. I wondered why there was no sign of bears or other creatures using this cave.

After digging for about two hours and through four or five yards of black sand, I noticed little flecks of what I wondered could possibly be gold but dismissed it as not. How could there be that much gold in no more than that much sand? I pulled the sand out on the flat area and spread it out. The opening got wider as I dug it out of the bottom part. Pretty soon, I had dug a hole five feet high and seven feet wide at the bottom. I went in sort of bent over and entered a cavern about eighteen feet wide by twelve feet high and maybe forty feet long.

On my left side facing in, the wall went straight up maybe twelve or so feet then curved all the way over and down. I can see some light on the far front side, so there was also another entrance or area to the outside. It also sort of came to me that this might be a warmer place to be if I had to spend the winter here while it's minus forty or fifty degrees cold.

I spent the rest of the day digging. There was a narrowed down area maybe twelve feet wide that went on back maybe another ten feet then up at a very steep angle. I got the front dug out another two feet down. I now realized that if I was going to use this cave extensively, I would have to remove about two more feet on the floor area of the cave. It appeared there was at least that much more sand above the bedrock.

On closer inspection there were more like another six. Would I be removing gold? I could feel a strong breeze coming through my enlarged doorway and disappearing out the deep hole in the back. That air was being sucked in forcibly by something unknown to me as yet. Samson was growling a lot and whining. I gave him some dog food mixed with bummer lamb milk and some of the ground-up mama-bear meat. Even in death, she was giving him life.

The thought hit me then: even in death, Christ was giving me life. "Take eat. This is my body which is broken for you."[2] So I now live by the life of another. He died so that I might have life and life more abundantly.

The garden was growing beyond my fondest expectations. I dug out some small potatoes and had new potatoes and peas in a cream sauce. I had moose backstrap steak, better known as rib eye. It was at least twice as good as the best beef I've ever eaten. I had beans, peas, cucumbers, zucchini, crookneck squash, carrots, and beet greens already. There were pencil-sized asparagus shoots. I wondered if I could make room enough to take them into the cave for the winter. I plan to take all my critters in and maybe put them in the little back area.

I put the trees in some of the bigger stainless steel pots and set them in the greenhouse. It was mid-July now, daylight 24-7, and stuff was growing. I had cabbage that weighed over sixty pounds, cauliflower as big as large dinner plates and six inches deep, rutabagas that weighed over ten pounds. Where would I put all this food?

I watered my garden five hours a day. I used five-gallon pails and a stainless three-gallon with a braided fish tape rope tied to the bail. I would simply throw it over the side of the flat rock area, pull up a pailful of water and empty it into five-gallon pails, then take two of these at a time over and pour them out on the garden. Next year, I would rig up a hose from upstream to water with, but the garden was so demanding along with the other chores that I didn't have time.

When I went to feed the birds the next day, I had a surprise: a small pullet egg and a happy hen.

I took one of the wheelbarrows up to the cave and started digging out the floor area. If I had calculated it right, I would remove about 1,500 square feet, and if I could get ten square feet per wheelbarrow full, that would be 150 wheelbarrow loads. In twenty-four days, my floor area was two feet lower and the bench outside three feet higher. I had wheeled out 255 loads. Now I had to only go up five feet and go in the doorway that was eight feet back in.

---

[2] 1 Corinthians 11:24 (KJV).

The doorway was now eight foot wide and seven foot tall. I set up some lights with a couple of fluorescent grow lights. I built a doorway by cutting planks with a power saw. I made two twelve-foot-long-by-three-inch-by-three-inch boards and screwed them together longways to form an L-shaped trough twelve feet long. I screwed this to a log to lay the motor part of the power saw in to make a level guide. I would move it down two inches for a two-inch board or three-inch for three-inch and so forth.

It worked pretty good, but making lumber this way is pretty slow. I wound up with a doorway with two board doors three feet wide and six feet tall. I had a two-foot-square plexiglass window on one. The other side had a six-foot-by-six-foot window. That opening had a beveled crack about ten inches wide going on up about two feet. I put a piece of galvanized tin in it. I had found a roll of galvanized tin two feet wide and fifty feet long in one of the big containers across the lake. I cut out a six-inch-plus round hole in it for a stove pipe and screwed it to the top of the window frame. I wedged it into place against the rock.

Seems like God had me covered in all my carpentry work. He's a carpenter too, you know. A broken heart, a busted life is what I brought Him. He tore it all apart and nailed a piece within—I mean, a *peace* within. I have a friend who wrote a song that had those words in it. I had several of his cassettes and played them a lot.

I wheeled in one of the stoves and set it back in the right-hand side about twenty feet back then ran the stove pipe along the wall and hung it from some rebar that I had driven into cracks in the rock. It went slightly up and out, a regular stove pipe and elbow on each end. A six-inch aluminum pipe would collect heat and disperse it all along that side.

I took a tent floor mat and put it down on the front half where I would be living. I brought in my couch and recliner chair and the aluminum spool for a table and a couple of fold up chairs. I used some poles and flattened them on one side and made a four-foot-by-seven-foot bed. I zipped two of the sleeping bags together with two rubber mattresses inside. I had a really comfortable four-foot-by-seven-foot bed with a twelve-inch-thick mattress. Now I was ready to move in and set up housekeeping.

I built a wall with a door across the back hole so I wouldn't have a draft every time I open the front door. Talk about a man cave, this was the real McCoy. I cut and stored twelve cords of wood and stacked it in the back of the cave. I harvested the garden. I had over eight hundred pounds of potatoes, 350 pounds of carrots, eight hundred pounds of rutabagas, over one thousand ears of corn, and another forty pounds of shelled-out popcorn.

There was no smell coming from the plane cockpit. The maggots had taken care of that. I decided to get the bodies out and bury them. The pilot still had a wristwatch on his arm bone that was still keeping time and had an inset part that said 8-4-85. By my calculations, I now knew I was only two days off. I must have been unconscious for about a day and a half. I had gone out on the midday of May 12 and woke up in the night on May 13, but I was wide awake on the morning of the fourteenth. Well then I knew, and I now had a watch. The leather band was shot, but I could still use the watch, and it had a calendar of sorts.

I found a billfold on the seat under the other bones that had five thousand dollars in it and a driver's license with a picture that said it was somebody named Freedom Terwilliger. So this guy was a Freedom Terwilliger. It sort of rang a bell, but I couldn't place it. I remembered seeing a fellow that looked like that picture. I put the billfold in one of the mesh side pockets of the plane, money and all.

GETTING READY
FOR WINTER

I t was the fall of the year, freezing every night, and it was only August. I robbed the bees. I have put together eight eight-inch supers of ten frames each for the bees, and every one of them was full. They had only a few hundred feet to go to get to the thousands upon thousands of berry plants. I think they must have been lowbush huckleberries. They were tart, very sweet, and very tasty. The bees were coming from every direction, and some were so loaded down, they would miscalculate and have to crawl the rest of the way to the hive.

I couldn't get out with the quad or the RTV because of the lake and the steepness of the creek bed even though the creek itself was only about four feet wide and six inches deep. So I would take a canoe and go across and do little hikes. No canoe or skiff would hold up a quad or RTV, but, oh, you know what? Three of them would if they were made into one unit.

I got busy. I cut some four-inch poles and lashed three canoes together, leaving about three feet between them. I cut holes under the gunwales to run the lashings through. I sawed two-inch-thick planks and screwed them to the poles. When finished, I had a barge of sorts with a twelve-by-fifteen-foot deck. I tied the skiff to one side after getting the barge in the water. I made a couple of three-inch-thick, sixteen-feet-long gangplanks, tied off the barge, and drove the quad and the trailer aboard. It didn't even seem to faze the depth of the canoes in the water. I pulled the gangplanks aboard the barge, released the tie ropes, and started the nine-horse outboard motor.

I went across to where the peat bog was. I found a place where I can wade ashore, got the gangplanks in place, and drove the quad and the trailer ashore. Chance and Samson were swimming around, and up swim the ducks. There were twenty-nine of them so I had twenty-six babies. I couldn't feed them all, so how would they survive the winter? They were of the Muscovy variety. They can't quack, and they roost in trees.

I rode up the old trail to the rim top, turned right and out onto the prairie. Boy, it sure looked different now that the snow was all gone. Miles and miles of open country all covered with millions of those lowbush berry plants. I filled a couple of two-gallon Ziploc bags and was just standing there in awe when my peripheral vision caught movement.

I grabbed the .358 out of survival instinct. Then I saw them, just two at first. I grabbed the twelve-gauge shotgun, and then I sort of walked over that way on foot. Pretty soon, I could see maybe fifty ptarmigan and all running together. I pointed the shotgun into the middle of the flock and pulled the trigger. A skillet shot. I got nine of them. I cleaned them by taking hold of their feet and standing on their wings. You just pull up, and you get a clean bird, the breast with the back and legs still attached. You reach in with three fingers and clean out the innards. I took off the livers and gizzards and put the breast and giblets in a Ziploc bag and the rest in a five-gallon bucket.

I went back, got the quad, the trailer and the animals aboard, and went home. Would I really have to stay here this winter? I should try to get ready just in case. Tomorrow, I will try to harvest berries. I slept five hours. I had left the quad on the barge. I took twenty-five five-gallon pails with lids, a hair pick, and a four-foot-by-four-foot piece of plastic. I thought to myself, *I can rake off the berries onto the plastic then dump them into a bucket.*

I got started and soon learned it was not going to work. The berry plants were so thick that they were growing together. I pulled one and shook it, and off fell the really ripe berries. If I held the fruit end over the bucket and the root end off to one side, I could pull the plant and shake the really ripe berries off into the bucket. In ten minutes, I had a bucket full, and in four hours, I had twenty-five buckets full, and it was only ten in the morning.

When I got back, I took twelve of the buckets and the quad back then came and got the rest of the berries and the animals. Then I started making a fruit press. I took one of the heavy aluminum pots and drilled a bunch of holes in it with a one-inch drill bit. I set it on a six-inch-thick split plank. The grooves from the split would let the juice run out and into a big flat pan that was about six inches deep. I lined the pot with cheesecloth, and I dumped in five gallons of berries. I made a thick block that fit the top of an aluminum pot, put it on top of the berries, then put a stump piece on top of that. I loaded about five hundred pounds of rock in the bed of the RTV, backed it in place, put a twelve-foot-long pole under the bed and the top of the stump piece and used this lever to squeeze out the juice. I got about two gallons of juice out of five gallons of berries.

The next day, I poured all the squeezed-out berries onto a thir-ty-two-foot square piece of plastic to dry clear out. They were bone-dry in forty-eight hours. I put them in five-gallon buckets and stored them for critter food. I cooked down the juice and then poured that out and let the sun make fruit leather out of it. I had about twen-ty-five pounds of fruit leather out of one thousand pounds of berries. I dried some berries whole and had about twenty-five pounds of rai-sin-like fruit.

I began to realize that I could be here all winter. I had a lot to do to get ready. I sacked up the root crops from the garden and buried them in the sand back by the cave woodpile. I canned a lot of stuff. I wrapped the cabbage heads in cellophane and stored them in the back of the cave in some of the empty trunks. I saved all the outer leaves and stems and the cleaning refuse to feed the animals. I was very concerned if I would be able to feed them all winter. I would probably harvest the eight large supers of honey and just let the bees die. I wasn't looking forward to the long winter nights with nothing to do. I built an outhouse on the flat rock area and made a porta potty for the cave with a bucket under it. It was crude but necessary.

ALL HELL BREAKS LOOSE

I went to bed that night and couldn't sleep. Chance was very nervous about something, and Samson refused to come inside the cave. It was just past dark when, out of nowhere, came a deep rumbling. It shook the floor of the cave. I thought, *Earthquake!* It was a steady roar for about a minute or so and then stopped. I got dressed and went down to the tent to sleep.

The next day, I went into the back of the cave where the hole went in and then up. I took a couple of flashlights in case one quit on me. It sounded like that noise came from behind that door over the hole. I had never taken time to investigate where that hole went. I figured it was some sort of old lava tube that went up and up into nowhere. That hole went in about ten feet then up at about a forty-five-degree angle. I climbed up what I judged to be fifty or sixty feet. It was hard to climb because the floor of the incline was a sort of loose shale rock.

There was a stiff breeze coming in behind me. I had left the outer door open in case of bad air. I came out into the biggest cavern I had ever seen. With the biggest flashlight, I could see that this cavern was maybe 150 yards long and a hundred yards or so wide. The air smelled clean. There was black sand with those little flecks of gold in it all over the floor area. If that is gold, I told myself, I'm the richest man alive with nowhere to spend it.

There was a little cave to my right that went into a little cave room about twenty by twenty feet off to the left and up a bit from the big cave area. I shined a light back in there. There was a lot of heat coming out of there, and I could see a bubbling pool of hot water with its stream going away from me into a black hole. I deduced from all the moisture on the walls and the floor that this thing had just erupted and had caused all the noise. The reason no animals stayed in this cave was obvious.

I walked clear around the perimeter of this huge cave room. At the far-left end was another lava tube that went in about thirty feet, turned right, and started getting cooler as it went. At the far end, about two hundred feet in, there was frost on the walls, and it felt really, really cold. I went and dug out a couple of thermometers from one of the marked trunks. About sixty feet in, it was thirty-eight degrees, and at the end, it was minus five, so here is both a walk-in cooler or refrigerator and a walk-in freezer.

I pulled in six thirty-foot-long, six-inch poles and made two tripods about ninety feet apart. I put one of the power cords that had a light socket every eight feet, and I put one-hundred-watt bulbs in every other one. I started one of the four-hundred-watt generators, and it would light all four bulbs. This would be my winter workshop, and I could bring all the animals and the birds and the bees in here for the winter.

The whole area stayed at about fifty-eight degrees at floor level. I cut a lot of logs about ten feet long and stored them along the woodpile edge where I could pack one at a time whenever I went to the upper cave. I got enough to cut wood up in the big house, as I now called it. I also got some eight- and ten-inch ones to make lumber. It was very hard work packing a log up that incline, and I decided to split out some boards and make some stairs.

There was no shortage of wood or saw logs. The hardest part was getting them off the pile and up to my front door. I gathered up all my tools that I figured I would need: my table saw and the band saw, which had blades to cut wood or metal. The blades were about three quarters of an inch wide and eight feet long. It even had a little welder part so if you broke a blade, you could slip the broken ends into a slot, push a lever, the sparks would fly, and the blade was repaired. Then a little narrow sander belt on the back side to smooth out the weld.

I had several boxes of blades for metal or wood. It would cut up to about ten inches thick. I had the hand planer and a couple of drill motors. I would have a complete shop when I got it all set up.

There were several storage batteries and lots and lots of wire. There were lots of small twelve-volt-size light bulbs that used very little energy. I could charge these batteries during the day off another four-hundred-watt generator and burn a taillight-size bulb at night. This would shatter the dark.

My eyes were still very good, and I could read with this much light. If I ran the generator four hours a day, I could keep the batteries topped off on a pint of gas every three days for a night-light. I knew the plane probably had batteries to start the engines. It turned out there were two 8D high drawdown batteries in the wing next to each engine. Another two were under the floorboards just behind the cockpit. There were also pulleys and pulley belts and so forth for repairs and two large repair manuals about three inches thick. I could use these in my outhouse along with the two catalogs I had found in one of the marked personal trunks.

It was not so long ago, I would tread out through the snow, then I'd set me down to rest like a snowbird in his nest. I'd sit and read the Sears and Roebuck catalog. Shakespeare? No, Little Jimmy Dickens. I got all this stuff packed into the big house, even the bees that I put way down in the far corner. I made meat poles and shelves in the cooler and freezer. I got all my meat in and frozen. I left the bees with two supers of honey and rendered the other six. I had ten gallons of honey. I went on one more trip to the berry field and got some berries to freeze. I found a whole hillside full of strawberries.

Up toward the top of this area was a whole hillside of white powdery-looking stuff. Turns out it was limestone, a whole mountainside of it. What a find! Now I would have all the soil sweetener I could use, and I could use it in my outhouse to keep the smell down.

I scraped together a five-gallon pailful and picked a few strawberries. I pulled a lot of strawberry plants. I thought maybe I could make a container bed and between the fertile soil and selecting the best plants, I could get bigger berries. The berries on these plants were only about one quarter inch across and maybe a half inch long. I loaded it all up and went home. I packed about two yards of peat moss up into the big house along with a bucket of lime and six buckets of pumice. I had a lot of chicken and turkey manure that I had piled up from the pens, and I packed in some of that. I made up a planting mix and piled it all up just to sort of let it marinate together.

I went out into my woodlot and split a lot of boards out of the bigger logs. I just split out the centers about three inches thick and ten feet long. This left the refuse in the field, and I had only to pack in the planks this way. It saved a lot of power saw chains and fuel. I had to cut all the corners I could to save on gas and diesel fuel. I can clean up the ends and edges with the power planer and make a lot of stuff I would need.

I built some pens for the animals out of split rail and small poles set about three inches apart for the birds. I took down the plastic over the garden and stored it. I got the skiff and the other canoe and put them under the overhang. I put big rocks on everything so the wind wouldn't blow it away. Well, I guess—no, I hope—I'm ready. Most of the time, I just called Samson *bear* because it was easier.

LIFE GOES ON

I was down on the flat rock with a campfire going and just enjoy-ing the evening when three bull moose came out on the far side of the lake, all spikes or bulls and about eighteen months old. They were young, tender, and fat. I shot all three. I needed meat, and I needed tallow. The dog and bear would need meat also, and the rest of the critters needed more protein in their diet. I got the canoe out of mothballs and went over and butchered all three and got it loaded and back to the flat rock area. I took the hides back over and put them in the peat bogs, where it was wet. I wanted to see if the tannic acid in the peat would help tan the hides, and it would loosen the hair so I could scrape it off.

I put the stomachs and contents into the stainless buckets and let them freeze. They were tapered so I could just dump them out, and it was cold enough to keep them outside. I could leave them there and bring one in at a time to feed the critters. I would let Bear and Chance chew a bone and then dry and pulverize them into bone meal. I gave bone meal to the chickens to make better eggshells and put it on the garden to add calcium to the soil. I put together some poles to stretch and work the hides on. Long story short, when I was done, I had the best leather I had ever produced.

I got all the meat cut up and in the freezer. I kept all the steak for myself and fed the rest of the critters. The critters that were meat eaters (pigs and chickens) were easy because they would eat anything you put in front of them, even garbage. I got the freezer and cooler shelves up and situated them then built stairs out of split lumber. I also built a bed for horseradish and one for asparagus and strawber-ries. Then I built some three-by-three-by-four-foot-deep containers for the trees. I would run a piece of cable around the top and bottom and winch it tight and clamp it with cable clamps.

I made some two-foot-by-two-foot-by-three-foot-deep barrels and dug up my sacks of root crops and transferred them and reburied them. I wheeled in all the trees clear out to the back. I hooked Samson up with a rope and made him pull the wheelbarrow through the sand, one tree at a time. I made two tables, eight feet long and four feet wide with a three-inch-thick top so I had a worktable sixteen feet by four feet. I made a smaller table to put the table saw on and another one for the band saw. I needed a better table for my living quarters, so I made a tank seven feet long with three lids side by side. It was thirty inches wide and forty inches deep.

I had a tub underneath. I planned to run hot water from the hot spring above and down to my man cave.

I needed a refrigerator in the man cave to keep things cold, so I took one of the trunks, set it on end, and put a couple of shelves in it. I made a stand and set it against the window with a two-inch-by-eight-inch slit in the window to match the two-by-eight-inch slit in the aluminum trunk back and screwed it all into place. The top shelf in front of the hole kept that area frozen and a couple of holes drilled into the boards for the lower area kept things cool. So now I would only have to go into my walk-in storage area about once a week.

I built a fire in the big house one day and sat down to eat my lunch when I noticed the smoke would go up, hit the ceiling, then follow along, and go out the upper left hand back and disappear like some giant chimney. I would have to build a long ladder so I could get up there and look into that depression.

CHRISTMAS DAY

I didn't have a calendar for next year, only my watch, so I spent Christmas Day making one. I had cut a small evergreen tree three feet tall and made a little Christmas tree and a string of popcorn on some monofilament that I took off a fishing reel. I made a moose loin roast and mashed potatoes and gravy, cut up some carrots, and made a blueberry cobbler. I was an accomplished cook. I had cooked for up to 180 people at church camps and a couple of summers on a fish tender. I kept a lot of recipes in my head if they hadn't leaked out through that cut I got in the crash. I kept a sourdough starter going all the time and made bread and cinnamon rolls weekly.

By the middle of February, I was taking a hot bath almost daily. I also use this tub to wash my clothes, and I had some large pans to wash dishes in. I built a dump box on the end of this to throw out used water. I had a drain that went out down into the sand and clear out to the creeks edge. It all had a Y-valve so I could empty the tub and then bring in new water.

In the big house, I had found a crevice in the rock toward the very back. It was about twenty feet up, and I could see back in it from the top of the orchard ladder with a flashlight. I could see a pool of water, maybe four or five hundred gallons. There was water dripping from the ceiling, and it must have emptied out the back somewhere because there was nothing coming out the front. I would later run an inch-and-a-half pipe from there to a tank because I had yet to make a tank for the critters, then I ran the pipe under the sand and all the way down to my man cave. This was clear, cold water—really, really good-tasting water. Now I wouldn't have to pack in water for me or the animals.

I needed a haul box on the front and back of my ATV. I decided to do that next. I made a box about ten inches deep, eighteen inches wide from front to back and as wide as the bike was across. I put a two-inch-high perimeter piece around the top lid and a piece of moose hide with the hair still on for Chance to ride in. I had tools stored inside and a thing called a lead sled to put on top if I needed.

I could put my .338 Lapua on this and cradle it and adjust it all so all I had to do was hold it against my shoulder, fix my sight, and pull the trigger. That caliber of rifle had been used by the army to make sniper kills of over two thousand yards. I built another for the back a foot deep, twenty inches wide for my tent and survival gear in case I ever broke down or something and had to spend the night.

Somebody had thought of almost everything but not quite. I had over two thousand paper plates and cups. There were forty-four stainless steel food trays about twelve inches wide by sixteen inches long with little dividers built in to keep food separated. I use these all the time to eat off and would wait till I had several dirty dishes before I would do them. There was no silverware, metal, or plastic. I carved out a wood spoon. I had my hunting knife but no fork, so I would stab stuff with the point of the knife to eat with. It was awkward, but I got used to it.

VALENTINE'S DAY

Valentine's Day came and went. I missed my sweetheart. Did she ever think of me? I knew I had kids but couldn't remember what they looked like. I couldn't remember what my wife looked like. I would have many dreams where I would see children and a woman. She was always leaning over the corner of a tall chest of drawers and just staring at me. Well, she would be sure I was probably dead, so she was probably married again.

What I did have was Jesus. He would come by every day. He would fill me with his presence. I would go into the holy of holies and sup with him and he with me. I would pray in the Spirit, and I would pray with understanding, just like Paul said. He would fill me with his joy and strength and love. My everyday routine was that. When I woke up, I would lie there and pray for a while, asking God for guidance and strength. He had provided in abundance my every need and then some. He was always there for me, teaching me, helping me.

My New Refrigerator

I built a wall across the last thirty feet of the cold tunnel. I took out the old poles and shelving and put in new ones that were better organized and stronger. Then I had a large area where it was just cold but not freezing. I made another wall on either end of my cooler area and made all new shelves and got them better organized.

I supposed Samson was hibernating somewhere, but I didn't know where. There was a little back inlet where the tunnel turned right, and there, he was sound asleep.

BEAR NECESSITIES

S amson was getting rough to play with, and he sometimes had a temper. I decided to try to fix that—fix him, I mean. I got some starter fluid to use as ether. I put it on a rag and over his nose. He tried to wake up and then went out for good, and I made a eunuch out of him. It should calm him down. Yes, I felt bad, but if I left him a bore, he might get mad and hurt or kill someone, someone like me. Now by the time he woke up, he would be all healed up.

This summer, I plan to train him to work, make a harness, and pack bags and training time. It was the first day of May. I have been here for almost a year in this savage wilderness.

THE GROTTO

I built a forty-foot-long ladder. It was eight feet across the bottom for stability and three on top. I got it worked up the end and propped up so the top edge was right on the top lip of where the smoke went out. Sure enough, I found a little niche tucked back in that I could get through if I sort of did a crunched-over walk.

The next day I took the .358 and a small shovel and went to investigate the tube that led away. About fifty feet in, it opened up to about twelve feet around. It went north at a slight upgrade. Three hundred feet later, there was a split that went to the right, and I could see a light about fifty feet away. I would look at that later.

I went another two hundred feet and broke out into a grotto, maybe one hundred feet wide and that far back in. I heard bleating and rustling. I saw the last of Dall sheep just going out of sight. This must be a winter shelter for them and has been for hundreds, maybe even thousands of years. The sheep manure was deep on the floor area. I dug down six or seven feet and still hadn't hit bottom. From the way it was sloughed off on the front edge, it was probably about twenty feet deep. There was more fertilizer here, more than I could use in fifty years of farming. After the first top foot it was just black crumbly soil and the top was fertilizer *ordinaire*.

I walked out on the front side as far as I figured was safe and looked out into a huge sunken valley enclosed by walls from seventy to three hundred feet tall. Some of the trees below had tops that were as high as the front of the grotto. The closer ones were the tallest and far bigger in circumference, fourteen to twenty inches in diameter with very little taper. I could see what appeared to be a frozen water-fall clear across on the north side of the valley, probably two or three miles away. I had brought my fifteen-power Swarovski binoculars but had left them back in the cave.

I went back to where the lava tube had split, turned left, and went up this Y about fifty feet and broke out upon a hillside over-looking a vast plain that fell away to the tree line a mile or two away. Off to my right and to the south of where I stood, I could see what appeared to be a creek valley. I figured the lake I lived on to be just west of there just barely out of sight.

I went back down the tube and got my quad and dump trailer. I had made sideboards for both trailers. Now I could get a full yard of materials on either if the weight didn't prevent it. I went off the ramp end and down the open side of the creek bed that emptied out of the lake. In about two hundred yards, I saw a place where I thought I could get up through the willows and on to that open hillside, where the lava tube exit was. I picked my way around snowdrifts and spent about an hour getting brush and other debris, rocks, moss, and so forth out of the entrance.

The quad and trailer went in easily enough, but I could see the RTV was too tall. I disconnected the trailer and used the blade on the front to loosen and pile up the manure. I had to load it by hand. It was dense enough. I could use the cob fork, and I had it full in less than ten minutes.

I got out ten more loads that day, so over twenty-one yards, and the next day, I took both trailers and got out forty more. Over half of it was that crumbly deep-down-black soil that was fully composted. It would probably grow stuff with no additives. I already had enough for this year and then some.

The warm air that rose out of the big house came all the way through and caused it to be ten or twelve degrees warmer in the back part of the grotto than in the front, so the animals would bed in the back, and the manure was about ten feet deeper in the back then in the front. It sure didn't smell like freshly baked bread.

I had started some tomato and pepper plants under grow lights. I would squeeze the water out of the soil I started the tomato seeds in. They wouldn't germinate in soil that was too wet. But the peppers are just the opposite; they want it soggy wet at about ninety degrees, and they come right up. I started them forty days earlier than the tomatoes, and they were already out growing the peppers. I ripped out some boards half an inch thick and four inches wide and eight feet long and put a spacer board every four inches. So in effect, I had a string of four-inch pots eight feet long.

I mixed soil, one part peat moss, one part compost, one part sheep manure, one part sand, one part pumice, and one pound of lime to a wheelbarrow full. It proved out to be an excellent starter mix and the plants grew rapidly.

By now, I had planted the cole crops, and they were ready to be transplanted into four-inch pots. After I planted them into the garden, I would have small cabbage and heads of cauliflower and broccoli and asparagus in about three weeks.

More Power

I had used one of the smaller chain falls and a long pole contraption with the bottom of the pole buried in the sand. I used this to lift the water pipe that went over into the spring. It erupted every eighty-seven days, and I had to pull the pipe out to keep it from getting torn up. I could put it back in and have it working again in about thirty minutes. I was going to put a lot of corn in this year—sweet corn and popcorn. Popcorn makes the best cornmeal.

I was also going to flatten more area and plant some hard wheat for flour, and I had some pearl barley that I had bought to eat, but I wanted to see if I could get it to grow, so I wanted to put in a row of that, a row being sprinkled seed over a foot wide by thirty feet long. That will produce a lot more grain than you might think. I could use my little hand mill and grind enough flour for a loaf of bread in about fifteen minutes.

I still had a little time before the thaw, so I decided to try to hook up the alternator from the plane to charge batteries with. I started by building a thick board tray of sorts with foot-high sides, and the whole apparatus would be mounted on that. Then it would simply have to be moved down the stairwell and out onto the flat in front of the door.

Water from the rushing creek piped into it, so it turned a waterwheel. I took the fish tape off the spool. It took me two days, and there were over forty miles of it. I put wood panels across the inside of the spool mounted against either wall of the spool. I took the self-aligning bearings off one of the carts over in the big aluminum containers. I used one of the bigger V pulleys to attach to the wood round I had mounted to the wheel that went through the center of the waterwheel. The wood was screwed to the metal, and an all-thread bolt went through the hole I had drilled through the axel. So as the wheel turned, it turned the axle and that, in turn, turned the big pulley that was connected the same way and a V-belt to turn the alternator and the wires from the alternator to the batteries. The alternator had a regulator built into it so it wouldn't over charge the batteries.

Then on the far end, I built a stomp mill out of pipe and a couple of sledgehammer heads. I had seen a similar device in a mining museum to bust up and pulverize gold-bearing rock. I would use it to pulverize bones and horns. Also, I could use it to pulverize limestone. I had used a power saw to drag through the limestone and granulate it. Now I could knock out the stuff between the cuts and pulverize it. I could keep the batteries all topped off and have lights all the time by hooking up the five-thousand-watt inverter. This would let me use my AC tools without having to start my generator. This would save me a lot of gas. I would have to wait till the spring thaw was over and the creek was running steady before I could try it out.

I made an eight-foot-high-by-two, two-foot-wide set of shelves just to the left of the top of the stairwell and twenty feet long. It could be reached from either side. I could store tools and parts on it so I could find them easier.

It was getting nice out, lots of sun. I cleaned off the snow from the big flat rock area with the blades of the ATV, just pushed it over the side onto the lake. I got the greenhouse plastic back in place and cleaned out and refilled the potato growing area. This time, it was fertilized with sheep manure. I tilled the soil with the Troy-Bilt and added more mix and fertilizer. I had rich deep soil and could put rows closer together for more production. I put my sweet corn on one end and popcorn on the other so they wouldn't cross pollinate. There were hardly any weeds in any of it. Understand that you have to keep the weeds out.

I had started some sweet corn in my four-inch board pots and transplanted them when they were about a foot tall. This gave about a thirty-day jump on the first roasting ears. I set up a stove on either end to burn at night to keep it from freezing.

I had made ten trips to the plane for gas this winter and two of the bladders were empty. I had started on the third. I would have to slow down on consumption if I was going to have to stay here many years. That would be possible if my charger worked. I wanted to get a sawmill set up this summer and saw a lot of lumber to have on hand for projects for the summer and next winter. By using it instead of a power saw, I would save a lot of gas, and I could mill about ten times faster. I hand pulled the generator charger or actually held it back and let it slide down the stairwell area and stored it on the flat at the bottom. There was a blade sharpener for the sawmill, and I built a table to mount it on.

ALWAYS READ THE MANUAL

I needed a supply of wood logs, so I got into that log pile and cut out a lot of the bigger ones and pulled them up to the flat. In five days, I had enough to cut about twelve thousand lineal feet of cants. I had some forty-foot ones I cut with a power saw on two sides. I leveled them on the flat area and stabilized them in place with holes in the rock and rebar driven through and into the hole. Then I lag-bolted the sawmill track to these. I made a tripod and lifted the sawmill head on to one end and got it set up on the track. I fueled up the eight-horse Kohler engine, then I got the manual out and studied it from cover to cover. Always read the manual from cover to cover. It will guide you and help you not to make a lot of life's mistakes.

The sawmill had a five-gallon fuel tank and a five-gallon water tank to drip water on the blade to help it slide easier. It had a ratchet lever and a scale to set the thickness of the board, dogs to hold the logs in place while they were being cut, and a log turner that you used to roll the log around with. To cut the log, you simply pushed the carriage down the track and cut off one piece at a time. When you had the log squared up you could cut it into the dimensions you wanted or lay the cant aside for further use.

I cut cants the rest of the day, and by the end of the seventeen-hour day, I had over two thousand board feet of cants cut. A board foot is twelve inches wide, twelve inches long, and one inch thick. I had used three gallons of fuel. Over the next two weeks, working only spare time, I cut another eleven thousand square feet. I had used thirty-seven gallons of fuel, and it would take another ten to cut these into finished lumber.

I love to work. I mean absolutely love it. I love to fish. I love to hunt. I love to trap. But if I could choose only one, I would pick work as my favorite.

The thaw would come anytime now. I wanted to get the fuel bladders off the plane just in case. There were five of them still full. I tried hoisting them with a come-along but couldn't lift them high enough to get them onto the bed of the RTV or even onto a dump-cart. I finally settled on an idea. I made a travois with the top part in the back of the RTV and hoisted the bladders onto the bottom. The bottom tips of the poles were the only part that hit the floor or ground. I got the five all off in about another hour.

Samson hadn't woken up yet. I let him sleep. I checked on him daily as he was basically shut in.

THE TEMPORARY TENT

I decided to replace the tents with a wood structure. Tents are temporary. *The tabernacle that housed the law dwelled in a tent of skin. This skin tent that I live in is the tabernacle of the Holy Ghost.* I had more than enough lumber. I laid it all out thirty by forty. I made two-by-fours. I made shakes for the roof. I cut siding boards to go lengthways. I would raise one side of an eight-inch cant so the board would be cut three quarters of an inch on one side and one quarter of an inch on the other. Then I dropped it back flat and cut straight across. When you factor in the thickness of the blade, I would get fifteen boards per cant. That one cant would make three quarters of one wall.

The roof shakes were half an inch thick and four-foot-long boards. You put them on starting at the bottom. You nail on one row with the nails across the bottom about six inches up, then a second row to cover the cracks of the first. The nails going through the top of the first covered the nails on the bottom and right on up. Each row covered three feet, and there were four sets of rows to the top on each side, and the topcap was two eight-inch boards nailed edge to edge.

I made the doors that opened out from the middle, so I had a doorway eight feet wide and eight feet tall. The hinges were eight-inch strap hinges, of which I found thirty-six. I used four of them and put a three-by-six plexiglass window on each end and two in front. The back wall of the building was against the wall on the back of the overhang, so it didn't need any windows.

I had a nice-looking thirty-by-forty-foot building. I put everything but the sawmill inside and all but two of the fuel bladders. I decided to make a cover from the back of the airplane to the wall next to my cave doorway. I wanted to get from my cave to the plane without having to wade through the snow in the winter. I had it all started in three weeks with a boardwalk to walk on or drive on.

I Go to the Valley

I had a little time, so I went scouting. I was afraid to take the quad on the ice, so I pulled a canoe to a point around from the ramp and out around the rock outcrop. I had the power saw and a grub hoe and my .358. I cut a swath through the willows and grubbed out the roots. Now I wouldn't have to go so far down the creek and then back up to the sheep gate.

I walked up to the top of the ridge until I was standing on the brink of the valley. I began searching the whole area with the Swarovski binoculars. This huge valley had no apparent way in or out. I spotted four grizzlies and sixteen moose. Some of the cows looked heavy with calves, as did the many sheep scattered upon the cliffs. There was steam spewing from the cliffs in literally thousands upon thousands of places. Everywhere there was a little soil for the roots; there was green showing.

The waterfall was beginning to trickle. I decided that spring in this land was as much as one month earlier than down on the lake just because of the heat in the cliff walls of this valley. I could see a hill to the east that was maybe a mile and a half away. It was perhaps two hundred feet above the valley floor. There were trees around the bottom to maybe a third of the way up, and then the rest was all green grass. There appeared to be a huge flat area on top and one lone tree growing out of the center. There had to be heat under that hill also.

I contemplated making another rope ladder and climbing down the eighty or so feet to the valley floor. I said to myself, "I will kill a yearling lamb and have lamb chops and/or roast leg of lamb." I was hungry, and that sounded so good. I will feed upon the lamb for renewed strength. I went back up the ridgeline and then off to my right and down into the streambed that went steeply on down and ran close to where my man cave was.

As I went slightly down, I came to the creek bank. If there had been water in the creek, it would have been straight down about forty feet between two walls four or five feet apart. I could see past the corner of the wall that kept me from going into the valley. There was a thirty-foot drop—actually, another waterfall that fell into the narrow creek between the two walls. If there was no other way out, this was very effectively a closed gate to this valley.

There was a short flat place on my side before the edge and another one on the far side that went ever widening back into the valley. If I could get a little bridge across at an angle toward the valley, I would have a road into that valley. An animal—or even a man, for that matter—could jump across that channel, but if he slipped and fell, it would mean certain death, and it wasn't worth it.

I went back home and picked out six six-by-ten-by-ten-foot-long sawed timbers. I packed them to the edge of the stream one at a time all the way from down below. I tied a fish tape to each one and then a stick onto the other ends and tossed it across to the other side. I made another braided rope. Each piece had a breaking strength of 1,600 pounds, but there wasn't enough bulk to hang on to. I wasn't comfortable with that little string. In fact I wasn't comfortable with rappelling down that cliff at all but figured I had to. I had an end of the fish tape tied off to six different small trees and had made me a sort of harness seat, but it still took all of my courage to go backward over the side.

I made it down okay. I was in a valley with at least four grizzlies and no gun. I should have tied on my Redhawk but didn't want anything that might hang up on something. I crossed over this part of Jordan and was in the land of the Philistines, but God would protect me, just like he did Israel and David. I was reminded that when David was in Saul's war room, he told Israel how he had killed a bear and a lion with his bare hands and then said this uncircumcised Philistine is no different. David was calling forth the covenant that God had made with Abraham, and that covenant was sealed in circumcision. David was saying, "I'm under covenant. He's not."

That involved shedding of blood and the cutting away of the flesh. I am under a blood covenant with Christ, and he has admonished me to separate myself from fleshly ways. My heart is circumcised, oh God.

I was on the other side. I pulled the timbers across one at a time and laid them side by side. I now had a little bridge, thirty-six inches wide and ten inches thick. I lashed them together so they wouldn't separate or fall apart as I walked across. I was full of joy and so happy that God had used a part of this incident to reveal his covenant to me.

NEW LIFE

S till no thaw. Seemed like it was later than last year. I got some wood together and built a partition for the back of the plane with a door in it. I had it closed with the ramp door for the winter and had to go in the front door, which involved going up and down the ladder. I didn't want to go on the ice lake again, even to walk.

I got started on a cover for the walkway from the front door of the cave all the way to the back of the plane. It was high against the wall and would shed the snow off into the creek bed. I had built a long sloping ramp from the fifty-foot-long flat to where it went down steeply to the creek. This ramp platform came out at the top edge of the rock flat area and would keep me from having to wade in water to get from the cave to the flat rock area or vice versa.

Then came the thaw. I still had a big part of the long shed to do, but it was a part-time project I could work in and on at any given time. I stayed inside and worked during the thaw. It was raining hard and blowing hard and was just plain nasty out.

On the fifth warm day, the sun came. The lake was ice-free. I got the barge back in the water. I loaded some lumber on the trailer of the RTV and my tools, screw guns, generator, and so forth and went up and started finishing my bridge. I had it done in two days of steady work. I now had a husky seven-foot-wide, ten-foot-long bridge ten inches thick. I made a secondary deck on it of two-by-ten boards that went out to form an approach ramp.

I rode all over the valley. I was wide-eyed in amazement. It was so beautiful, and everything was new to me. I must have been a sight to see: long hair, long beard, tacky clothes, but I bathed regularly and would hack off my hair and beard periodically with my hunting knife.

I wandered over near the sheep grotto. Manure had been trampled over the front edge, and the area at the foot of the cliff was probably twenty foot deep and tapered and thinned out down to thirty feet out. This caused the trees to grow taller and bigger in girth. Some of these trees were two feet through and over one hundred feet tall and had very little taper. I would bring the saw mill up here and mill this much better lumber from now on.

OVINIA

I heard a noise and grabbed the .358 rifle. There was a sheep to my right on the cliff and looking at something below—a grizzly maybe? I went over cautiously and ready. A baby lamb had fallen into a pocket in the rock and broke a front leg. To leave it would mean certain death. If a critter didn't get it, the elements would.

I picked up the little female lamb and took her home with me. Chance was running alongside and looking up at us. I'm sure he was jealous, but he would get over it. I got some milk in her and made a splint and set that leg. Everywhere I went, that lamb followed. I named her Ovinia the Ovine.

Samson finally woke up. When he saw the lamb, he started licking his chops. I tried to give him some hamburger meat, but he wouldn't eat it. I gave him some bummer lamb milk, but he didn't want that either. He started gnawing on a piece of wood. I remembered how that black bears back in Washington would lick sap and eat cambium bark off fir trees to get their digestive system going after the long winter sleep. I cut some three-inch-in-diameter twenty-year-old trees and stripped off the outer bark. Sure enough, he started eating the inner cambium bark. Two days later he was eating anything edible. I gave him a lot of old bear meat, his mother. Again, even in death, she was giving him new life.

I got the greenhouse put back together, tilled the soil, and put a wood stove in each end. I let all the animals and birds out of the cave. I put the beehive in the end of the greenhouse. The birds started scratching around, but I hadn't planted seed yet, so it was okay. The bees started buzzing around. The lamb was apparently going to be okay. She was getting around like nothing had happened. I took the splint off the little thing, and she went crazy, leaping and jumping all over the place. But why wouldn't she? She had just been set free. It was the "gate beautiful" for her.

It hit me then: what if she had a kid? Could I milk her and have fresh milk and butter and cheese? Just one of those thoughts, but it might work out.

PROGRESS OF A PILGRIM

The water went down. I sawed more lumber. I worked on my shed roof. I pinned up the pigs and birds and turned the ducks lose on the lake. What a farm I now had—E-I-E-I-O. Now where did that come from?

This summer, if they had offspring, I would try turning some loose in the upper valley. They just might be able to survive on their own. Later, I would try some turkeys also if I got them started reproducing. They could fly up onto the ridges and eat berries.

I got my newly invented waterwheel charger outside and a pipe coming down from upstream across the wall about forty feet above the cave door, then straight down, and followed the edge of the partition wall that separated and turned the stream hard right. On my cave side, it went straight out and down, so I ran the pipe down and put a twenty-two-degree elbow that fed the water right into my waterwheel and ejected it over into the creek's edge. It was a ten-inch pipe, so it was way more water than necessary. It spun that wheel way faster than needed and with more power. It worked better than my fondest expectations.

I had most of the dispensing wires all in place: to the cave, to the big house, down my new covered walkway, clear to the lower barn shed, and even to the plane. Now I would use the five-thousand-watt inverter to run all my power tools and other stuff I wasn't using before. I had that small microwave, a Bunn coffee maker, which had to maintain hot water all the time. So now, coffee every morning by Bunn.

One of Fred's boxes marked "Personal" had the coffee pot and the microwave in it and a midsize cuckoo clock. I set it up on a middle shelf of the shelves I had over by the woodpile. I had put my bear skin rug on the floor. I had a table and chairs, a bathtub with hot running water, plenty of wood, and a stove to cook on. I also had four gas stoves with two burners each and four gas lanterns, but they all use gas. I would use them only when I didn't have anything else. I had a stove and lantern in my box on the bike for light and extra heat if I needed it.

But my God shall supply all of your needs according to his riches in glory.[3] He certainly had provided my every need. He has prepared a table for me even way out here in the middle of the wilderness. I didn't have a TV or radio, no outside communication—just a still, small voice. His sheep know his voice, and they will not follow any other. Well, I guess I could learn to cluck, crow, hiss, growl, bark, bleat, or oink. Is that pig Latin? I felt richly blessed. I have plenty to do to keep me occupied.

Later, I needed to get in a lot more coal, moose, and sheep manure and explore the upper valley some more now that I could get a vehicle in there. I like to use moose manure; it releases its fertile value more slowly and steadily. It puts off heat as it composts. It's not that hard to find or pick up.

I wanted to try to empty and move one or two of the big aluminum storage sheds. I was sure if they were empty, they would float. I had found this contraption in one of the sheds. I didn't know what it was. It had three sets of steel rollers, one above the other, and powered by an electric five-horse motor or a ten-horse gas engine. There was no manual that I could find. I took it over and put it in my wooden shed building. I hoped I could figure it out. I had a hunch that it must have something to do with gold mining.

I decided to go exploring in the RTV again. I got the canoe barge back in the water and tied off, loaded the RTV and tools that I thought I would need on it. I only had to go less than sixty feet and again tie off the barge and unload it.

We—I mean Chance, Bear, and Ovinia—spent the day in the valley. We rode all over the place and saw twenty-two moose, two bears, and more sheep than I could count. They had a unique feeding

---

[3] Philippians 4:19 (KJV).

system. Some would go high on the cliffside and watch, while others would venture out into the valley to feed. If a guard sheep would spot trouble, it would stomp its foot, and the feeders would scramble back to the safety of the cliffs.

I saw one bull moose that had a rack of horns that was beyond anything I could have imagined. It looked as wide as he was long. I had no desire to kill him. He was magnificent just to look at. A trophy for sure, but when I could see him in his own element, it was so much more rewarding.

I also saw a huge Dall ram. He had a full curl set of horns. He was apparently very old and limping. I thought after glassing him that one back leg was partly missing. He wouldn't make another year. I decided to take him for the meat, the hide, and that set of horns.

I laid the Lapua over the corner of the bed of the RTV. The range finder said 1,143 yards. The scope was calibrated out to two thousand yards, but I had never shot it over seven hundred yards. I dialed in the scope to 1,150 yards, held steady, slowly let out my breath, and squeezed the trigger. I had waited for him to be right on the edge of the little flat spot he was on about twenty feet above the valley floor so he would fall down where I could just drive up to him. I had lung shot him, and he had jumped back and stayed on the ledge. I would have to get up there to retrieve him.

I spent about two hours making a long ladder with rungs spaced about thirty inches apart. I got him down and skinned out. I bleached out the skull and hung it on the woodpile cover. It was beautiful. He was fifty-four and a half inches wide hornwise.

THE VALLEY
NOMENCLATURE

O n the north end, which was two and a half miles from the entry point, about one hundred yards from the west edge of the valley, waterfall lake, was another hot spring. It emerged from the wall about thirty feet up and fell into a pool of about twenty feet wide and forty feet long. It was a natural swimming pool but hot enough to cook you. It went into one end of the pool and followed along that wall and tumbled out the far end and down into a little flat bottom canyon that went slightly down and to the west then disappeared underground.

This north-facing wall was more in at the top than at the bottom. Not even a sheep could have traversed that wall. It dripped warm water the full expanse and the whole area of about four acres was covered in deep lush grass. The moose wouldn't feed in there because they could be trapped by the grizzlies. I thought, *Boy, what if I had a fence across the front and made this into a wheat, alfalfa, and corn field?* It was evident that it was rich subirrigated soil with natural heat under it. I would look into all that later, but it was too late for this year.

On further investigation, I found an area three miles from there in the southeast corner, where there was an old ravine that went out through the cliffs to the east. There had been a huge rockslide that had filled it in. This could have been an opening to the outside at some point, and the animals had come in that way. There were no wolves that I ever saw, but there were a lot of lynx cats and arctic foxes. I would have to get them under control if I expected the ducks and turkeys to survive.

The next two weeks, I hauled and stockpiled coal on the far side of the lake over next to the peat bog. I could get it from there as needed after the freeze-up. I had to pickax it loose and then handload it. It was hard and slow work.

Then I got an idea. I got the rotary hammer out and a one-and-a-half-inch star drill bit and the generators. I made holes into the face of the coal seam about three feet apart, and up the side, about twenty feet, I loaded the holes with dynamite and turned the crank on the detonator device. I figured I rolled out at least forty tons. Now all I had to do was load it into the vehicles.

LIVER LIPS

Bear had disappeared when I blew the coal. He had been right near the coal, and I didn't see him when I set it off. I saw him running full bore up the hill behind it, but he never came around. I thought maybe he was hurt. I drove around looking for him, but he was nowhere to be found. Two weeks later, he showed up down on the flat rock area. He would have had to come down a steep hill and across the woodlot or swim across the lake to do that. I was glad to have him back.

I got out at least forty tons of coal and five square yards of limestone. I spotted a grizzly feeding on a moose and sort of drove over that way for a closer look. As I circled back, I almost ran over a newborn moose calf. The little thing was still wet and hadn't even tried to get up. The afterbirth was still attached to her. I pulled them loose and dried her off with a gunnysack. She started to try to get up, but I wanted to get out of there, so I cradled her in my lap and left. I bet she didn't weigh over thirty pounds.

I got her back and washed her with warm water and dried her off. I mixed up some bummer lamb milk, made up a bottle with the rubber glove finger trick, and got some milk into her. "Well, there you go, Liver Lips," I said. The name stuck.

I kept her isolated in the cave for two weeks and fed her every two hours day and night. It loved to play and run, and I would take her outside, and she would run and romp with the others. Bear still liked to roughhouse, and he knocked her down and held her down with one paw. She was screaming bloody murder, and I got over there and scolded him. He let her go and just sheepishly looked at me as if to say, "I was just playing." Thankfully, he had lost most of that aggressive, dominant mentality.

THE MIRROR

I was looking through the big metal trunk to see if there was any paperwork for that contraption. Sure enough, I found a large manila envelope that said, "Rock pulverizer machine." You simply fed rock that was under three inches in diameter into the top, and it came out the bottom in salt-size powder.

After going through the top rollers, it was about a quarter of an inch in size, then the second set broke it down to about one thirty-second of an inch size, then after going through the last one, it was a powder. Wow! I bet it would not only do rock, but it would also do salt or bones or limestone, and it would do it in a fraction of the time it would take my stomp mill, which would now be rendered obsolete.

I also found this picture of a beautiful Indian lady in her native clothing. It was a three-foot-by-four-foot portrait, and across the bottom was inscribed, "To my darling Freedom. Your wife, Anna *Little Bird* Terwilliger, 1935." So this was Fred's wife then. She had died trying to give birth to Freedom the fourth.

I remembered a man telling me about this and how he had never been able to stop grieving for her or the child. I now knew his name and associated it, but I still couldn't fit it into the situation I was now in. I took the picture frame and glass to try to make a mirror. I took the picture and rolled it up neatly and put it back into the trunk. I made a black paint out of soot and crushed up charcoal and mixed it with warm bear fat and painted it onto one side of the glass then put the pasteboard part back behind the glass and put it all back into the frame. It turned out great. Now I could see myself in the glass clearly. Long beard and long, shaggy hair—I felt like an unkept old mountain man. I wished I had some scissors, but I didn't.

I soaped my head and face down in lather and shaved my face and head bald with my hunting knife. I felt so clean and a lot cooler. I hung the mirror in the cave. I have plans to make a chest of drawers and would hang that mirror right above it.

Make Hay while the Sun Shines

I decided to go into that little offshoot valley and make some hay for next winter for the moose and sheep. I had that hand sickle, but I also had that power hedge trimmer with a long four-foot blade. If I could mount it on the front of the ATV and hook up a string to open the throttle and mow a four-foot swath at a time. I cut an acre and let it dry then loaded it on the RTV and hauled it down to the lake side and stacked it. I probably had seven or eight tons of really good-looking hay.

This grass, whatever it was, had a large seed head and would be high in protein. On one corner was a short grass that had nearly half the stem that was seed. It was very dark, nearly black, and looked like rye. I cut the heads off it and put them in a gunnysack to dry clear out then thrashed the sack against the rock to knock out the seed. When done I had a three-gallon stainless steel bucket nearly full.

I was going to try to grind it and make some bread and see how that tasted. In the end, I ground it, mixed it with wheat flour, made some little round loaves, and let it rise. I put it in a kettle inside a bigger kettle on the stove with a lid on the big kettle. I created a new and wonderful, tasty rye like dark-brown bread. I made some cinnamon rolls with blueberry-like raisins, and that was a new and wonderful recipe also.

I harvested the garden and canned a lot of tomatoes and other vegetables also. I had a lot of dried corn, both sweet and popcorn. I would grind the popcorn into a meal for cornmeal. It made the very best cornmeal for cornmeal mush, fried cornmeal mush, or cornmeal muffins. I made a large breakfast one morning of fried cornmeal mush, bacon, eggs, and moose calf backstrap. Now that's eating high off the moose.

I always ate well. I ate all the steak and made a lot of a front quarter into hamburger. Everything else was made into food for the critters. Meat is high in protein, and all animals need it, and meat was the best renewable source.

I also made a lot of soups, stews, and chili. All had meat, and all had tomatoes, so I made sure I had enough canned tomatoes. I snacked a lot in the evenings on crackers and cheese. I would run out of crackers. I had a recipe for soda crackers, but they never turned out as good as the store-bought ones.

This winter I plan to make a lot of different sausages, kielbasa, brots, salami, headcheese, regular link sausage and others. I had these recipes in my head. I had saved the small intestines out of the sheep and moose to stuff the meat in. I cut the intestines into lengths of about twenty feet. I washed them, strung them onto a wire, and pulled one end back over itself till it was inside out. Then I washed it, then I put several of them in Ziploc bags and froze them till I needed them. The small intestine of a large moose will make a three-inch-di-ameter stick of headcheese, bratwurst, liverwurst, bologna, so all I needed was the right stuff and spices, and I had all that also.

A Two-Season Year

S eemed like there were only two seasons here, summer and winter, and winter was again fast approaching. I brought in a lot of sawed lumber and split cants up into the big house, probably seven or eight thousand board feet, more than I would need for a winter project.

I put the saw mill cutting head in the new shed and covered the tracks with tarps and rocked them down. I got another twenty cords of wood brought in to add to what I still had left from last year. I probably had enough to last two years, but if I got hurt or something, I would have extra. Always pays to plan for the unexpected, my dad used to say.

I unpacked the Pelton wheel generator and laid it all out, then categorized it according to the schematic and manual. The generator was a two-stage affair, four-KW or eight-KW. KW is for kilowatt, and a kilowatt is a thousand watts, so eight KW is eight thousand watts, enough to run eighty one-hundred-watt light bulbs simultaneously. It takes half the water pressure to run a four-KW as it does an eight-KW.

This wheel was big for what it was supposed to do, but it could be used or driven by a thirty-foot head or pressure from thirty feet above. That same wheel would drive twenty-five kilowatts with a hundred-foot head. The cups inside were four inches in diameter and four inches apart. The water entered through a four-inch nozzle and exited a quarter turn later.

There were four intakes and four exhausts and a gear reduction to cause the generator to run much faster than what the Pelton wheel turned. I plan to have it all ready to go by next spring. I already had the piping in place that would run it or the paddle wheel by adjusting a valve on each intake till the gauge reads 120 and then you adjust it till it fine-tunes the hertz also.

I found enough wiring to do three lodges, so I had wiring coming out my ears, wiring from fourteen- to eight-gauge, and plenty of light bulbs for both incandescent and fluorescent and a lot of specially made tube-type fluorescent grow lights four feet long.

GONE FISHING

I decided to go fishing before the lake froze over. I had seen fish rising and sometimes jumping clear out of the water. I tied off the skiff to the barge and pushed the barge out to a place on the northwest side. It was about 250 feet deep here. I had a chair on the barge and a couple of fish poles. I plan to put a chunk of liver on one and put it down and surface fish with a lure with the other while I wait for a bite on the other.

The bait no more hit the bottom than I felt a notable tug on the line. I waited a few seconds and the line was moving sideways. There was no breeze, so the barge wasn't moving. I set the hook. I could tell it was a fairly heavy fish. It fought hard for about a minute, and then I started bringing him in. I finally got it up. It was a burbot, probably eight or ten pounds. Burbot are freshwater lingcod. As far as I'm concerned, they are far better than any other lake fish, the exception being kokanee, which are landlocked sockeye salmon.

I didn't need more fish, so I put the burbot in the bottom of the skiff and went back to the flat rock. I would do this again sometime. When I cleaned him, his belly was full of prawns or freshwater shrimp. They were exceptionally large. I decided right then to make a shrimp trap. Using quarter inch rebar. I covered it with half-inch hardware cloth, baiting it with a chunk of liver.

I went back out and set the trap in, about where I had caught the burbot, and tied off the line to a plastic jug. I plan to let it set for a couple of hours before I check it. Then I moved over and again got my heavy rod with a one-hundred-pound braided test line baited up with two large prawns and let it down. Sure enough, I hooked something and brought in another burbot, about a five-pound one. I unhooked it and put the hook through its middle back and put on a larger weight. I thought maybe, just maybe, there might be a thirty or forty pounder down there.

I got it almost down, and the line tightened; the reel started going and the pole bent. I loosened the drag so I could hold on to the pole. It stopped moving, and I couldn't get it to move. I knew it had to be a fish and a big one. It felt like the big halibut I had once caught. I tapped the pole with the inside of my hand, and nothing happened. Finally, after steady pressure for two hours, the thing started moving and down apparently into deeper water. Then he just started coming up—slow but still coming.

Every once in a while, he would make a short run back down, and I would work him back up. Finally, after a four-hour battle, I had him alongside—no camera, what a fish! He was over half as long as the canoe side of the barge, so that would mean fifteen feet of barge, and that fish was somewhere around eight feet long. I'm sure it was a burbot. I didn't know what to do with him, so after admiring him a bit, I took out my hunting knife and cut him loose. Acids in a fish would dissolve the hook, and he would be fine.

It was getting dark. I skipped the shrimp pot and went home to bed. That fish had flat worn me out. I tried to sleep, but every time I closed my eyes, all I could see was that fish.

When it got daylight again, I went out and pulled my shrimp pot. It was jam-packed full of jumbo prawn. "Prawns and fries tonight," I said to myself. I cleaned and froze the whole lot of them. If I wanted fish, I could go cut a hole and fish through the ice. These were all wild caught in cold water, and they were delicious.

NEVER-ENDING CYCLE OF WORK

I dismantled the greenhouse and stored the other machinery, hoses, and garden tools in the shed with the RTV and ATV and any tools I didn't figure to use this winter. I got all my critters back up into the big house along with the bees. I now had two hives as they had swarmed, and I caught the swarm. I had sixteen supers of honey of ten frames each. I needed to extract and get the frames ready for next year, a good winter project.

Liver Lips was now bigger than me by a long shot. I had trouble getting her to lead up the stairwell, but she finally did, and I brought in a lot of hay and some straw. I had a lot of corn and garden stuff also. Liver Lips would eat the corn, cob and all. I had cut all the cornstalks, and there were several hundred pounds of them. I froze them till I fed them, but Liver Lips thought they were candy.

Next summer, I would try to set some eggs and get some frying roosters to eat. The ptarmigan were good but bony, so I got to where I would just use the breast and use the rest to bait my lynx and fox traps. I had a lot of trapping to do. I would make a little covey beside a lynx run and put a ptarmigan bait in the back and a conibear trap in the front. I got twenty-seven lynx my first season and stretched and tanned the whole lot. I got a lot of grouse also and used them the same way.

I loved the work, and I would work long hours and try to spend at least two hours a day in prayer. I would say, "God, if I'm supposed to be your servant and work for you, how in the world is living here in exile supposed to accomplish anything?" He reminded me of John on the isle of Patmos, and he spoke to my inner man that he would accomplish his purpose in me in time. God works in time, on time, every time.

I was also enjoying life here so much. Sometimes it was like I was two people. One wanted to be rescued; the other loved this place and wanted to stay here forever. Sometimes I figured I would die here and no one would ever know.

ANOTHER DREAM

Your old men shall dream dreams. I must be getting old. That night, I dreamed I found a billfold with my name and picture on it. It was on the plane in the bottom of one of those net pockets on the far side of where I had set.

The next day, I trekked through the weather and down to the plane on my new walkway, which was now dry and bare of snow. I went in my new doorway and right over to the net pocket I had seen in my dream. Sure enough, clear in the bottom under some papers, I found a billfold. I opened it up, and there was a driver's license behind clear plastic with a picture on it. I got it out and looked at it close. It said Clint W. Terwilliger. It was the guy in the big mirror. "Me," I said. I must be Clint, and that's sure enough my picture, but it still wasn't clear to me. I was in sort of a fog.

I gathered up everything and took it back with me.

NEW LIGHT

I had light all over now that I had my waterwheel charger, but I would lose that when the creek froze up. The bigger need would be for the long winter night dark time. I wondered aloud if I could use the water I had piped down from the hot spring to turn the wheel. I got busy, and in less than a week, I had made the transition. The hot water would remain unfrozen until it was ejected into the creek bed.

I went back to investigate the rest of the stuff in my billfold and also read the old newspapers. Some of the magazines had pictures of trophies of different animals. There were some maps, and for a while, I thought maybe they could help me find a way out. Turned out they were maps of the Mackenzie River away north of where I was.

There were three trunks altogether that were marked "Personal, Fred." Two were the two by two by three and one was the big three by four. I hadn't opened one of the smaller ones yet. This paper said there was a cassette player and also an audio player, several movies, and several sets of gospel and Western music. I found this trunk and got it out and opened it.

There was also a small TV with a twelve-inch screen and a place to stick the movie cassette. There was another cuckoo clock—a bigger one—and, of all things, a small silverware set. It appeared to be real silver and was for six people. Now I had a real fork, knife, and spoon. I was elated. Funny how much little things count sometimes.

There were more tapes and movies. I already had some, but these were new and different. There were forty-seven song tapes and fifty movies. I started playing a song by Hank Williams, and Chance just looked at me and cocked his head and started howling. There was a non-Western movie called *O Brother, Where Art Thou*. I just about wore it out. I fell asleep watching it the first time and woke up on the couch feeling cold. I got up, dressed, built a fire, and got ready for another day.

MY WINTER FARM

I began building some long open bottom beds for indoor veggies and greens and so forth to have fresh all winter long. I would be using these about eight months out of the year. I made four of them four feet wide and eight feet long and one foot deep. I could get four of them in the twenty-by-twenty-foot area that was just in front of the hot spring area that was at the far end and to the left. I left a two-foot crawl space between them. I had chard, spinach, beets, onions, radishes, turnips, cukes, peppers both mild and hot, and a tomato plant.

Pepper plants will live over, and I had some that covered half of one container. I planted in succession so I would have a new crop coming on all the time. I finally got the timing and amounts of each right, so I didn't waste so much. It really wasn't wasted as I would feed it to the chickens, ducks, and pigs. I made all of these out of split wood that was about three inches thick. I also made two-foot-by-two-foot-by-two-foot-deep split wood containers for my blackberry and raspberry plants. I also had a huge stockpile of soil I had put together to just let it sort of marinate and be ready to use. I figured I probably had enough for six or seven years.

Christmas came and went, and a new year was born. Samson was fast asleep. I had put some straw in his little spot. He looked so peaceful just lying there, lightly snoring.

I spent the next two days getting the Pelton wheel ready to start up. I would place it on the right side of the area where I had the doorway going outward. There was about twelve feet over to the rock partition wall and about the same to the outside edge next to the creek. The wheel lay flat above its foundation, and the lower part collected the exhaust water and shot it over the bank into the creek bed some fifteen feet below.

The generator was about three feet above this with control panel and dispensing wires and so forth above that. It used up maybe a four-by-four-foot area and was out of the way, and there was still room enough for the paddle wheel charger alongside that on the far outer edge. If I ever got a shed roof finished back into the corner area, I had to form the shed roof around the downpipe. It would cover both of these and keep them all out of the weather.

If everything worked the way it was supposed to, it would use water from a ten-inch pipe that was already installed. It had about forty feet of drop right straight down and then a slight angle across the cave side of the rock wall where the creek turned. I divided the ten-inch head into four four-inch nozzles to feed it into the four intakes of the wheel. I would have to wait for the spring thaw to be over to start it up. I wanted everything to be completely ready to go. I had to pull the intake pipe up out of the creek so it wouldn't freeze and bust.

I had the chain fall hoist in place and holding it up and would only have to climb up there and lower it back into place. That little ledge it lay on was about two feet wide and ran along the wall all the way to where it cornered down at the flat rock. I had all the wiring in place for each area. I had outlets and switches installed where I would need them. I would have free electricity with no monthly bills. I felt really happy and gave myself a pat on the back.

I made a forge of sorts with billows made from half-inch-thick boards laid with a second layer crossways to hold it together. I filled all the cracks with pitch tar to seal it. I used moose hide for the collapsible part of the bellows. I had a piece of hide over a hole on the bottom side and a long handle with a rope up and over a pulley. This opened the billows, and the little piece of hide over the hole would let air suck in and then flap back shut, and all the air would have to go out the nozzle under the fire. I ran coal through the rock pulverizer and then mounded it over the fire part with a little open side. It would heat a half inch piece of rebar in less than three minutes.

I needed a plow. I cut out a piece of a quarter-inch-thick flat stock and heated it to white-hot and beat it into the shape of a plow-share. I made connecting pieces and bolted it all together so it would fit on the front of the RTV and could be raised and lowered with the winch. I could only turn over about six inches of soil at a time. It took me two days to plow two acres eight inches deep.

I went to the grotto and pushed a lot of the fresh top layer of manure over the front edge. I hauled it the two and a half miles to my field and spread it and tilled it in with the Troy-Bilt. I had a lot of hybrid seeds, but I also had a complete collection of heirloom seeds. I would let some of the heirloom plants go to seed every year so I would always have new seed for future crops. I had a tomato hybrid seed I used because I could get a good-tasting large fruit in only forty days in this long hot-days season.

Earlier this year, I had started to make a trackway up my stair-well for the RTV. I figured I could put weight on the front and hook up the winch so I could control it from the cab and then I could use that to take stuff in or out clear over to the freezer entrance. That would beat having to pack it.

Then I got one of those silly ideas I am so famous for. Why not make some pack bags and a harness for Samson and, later on, Liver Lips and let them pack stuff for me? I wanted to put in a thick plank gangway in the center with four-inch holes about an inch deep for traction for bear feet and moose hooves. I made a fresh air duct that went from the creek side under the sand across the outside area, then under the door, through the man cave, then emerged and went up the left side of the stairwell clear up into the big house.

I made the duct in ten-foot sections that were twenty inches square. I tapered them slightly so the one end slid into the next about six inches. It went back under the sand into the big house about fifty feet and surfaced again. I put a ramp up the center area between the stairs and the air tube. I made it out of eight-inch-wide planking that was eight inches thick by eight foot long. I still wanted to try to see if the RTV would go up also.

I made an anchor post at the top about fifteen feet in. I drove the RTV through the man cave, hooked up the winch for safety, and

I started up the stairwell. Long story short, I made it just fine. Now I would have to back it down and let the winch off as I went.

By the time all this was done, spring had sprung. It was time to stop playing around and get busy. I started by reinstalling the greenhouse plastic so the soil could warm up. I got the hot water running through the pipes. This helps tremendously. I got the potato bin refilled and replanted. I got my Pelton wheel in place and the water pipe reinstalled. I got it all regulated, and it did its thing. Now I had alternating current to the whole place.

A CLOSE CALL

I decided to go down to the grotto area and holler for Ovinia. I hadn't seen her for several days. I was a little worried. I hadn't seen any grizzly signs, but I wasn't sure I had got them all.

I wanted to check on some timber to cut next. I would do some measuring and check for rot or hollow trees. I got off the quad and went over about fifty feet to look at a big fir tree. As I stepped around it. I came face-to-face with a big bore grizzly. He laid back his ears, popped his jaws a couple of times, dropped down on all fours, and charged. I figured this was it. I had left my gun on the quad. All I could do was scream, "Jesus!"

There was a blur of fur, a lot of loud growling, and the next thing I could see was Samson and that big bore going at it about ten feet in front of me. Samson had followed me like this, and I would never know it unless I stopped for some reason, and he would catch up. He had hit that grizzly from the side, knocked him off his feet sideways, grabbed him by the throat, literally picked him up by the throat, rolled him over his shoulder and back, and body-slammed him on the ground. Then he held him there by the throat till he quit quivering. He was dead.

I saw the ground coming up to meet me. When I came to, Samson was licking my cheek. I just sort of said to myself, "Well, Lord, I guess you're not done with me yet." There's power in the name of Jesus.

ANOTHER CLOSE CALL

I wanted to do another scouting trip on foot where the ATV couldn't go. If I hurried, I could squeeze it in before I got too busy. I could go down the outlet creek trail for about three hundred yards, then the creek made a hard right turn and started down a little canyon that was fairly steep. All that wood on the outside corner kept me from going on down the outside, so I crossed over before the bend, went down a way, and then crossed back over to the other side where the going was easier.

I got up on the ridge side that went parallel about twenty feet above the creek. I could see a flat bowl a couple of miles away but couldn't see any water. I walked on down a little closer to the creek, where the going got easier at that level. All of a sudden, there was this awful smell. I started looking around. There were a lot of white bones bleached out by the sun and more that were a tannish-brown color and still more that still had red sinew on them, maybe chewed on this very day. I thought, *Lord, I'm right in this old boy's kitchen, and it's probably his breakfast time.*

I started looking around behind me. I slipped the safety off the .44 Ruger Carbine autoloader, and checked the .44 Redhawk revolver in my belt. I would look all around, move back a few feet, look again, move again, then look again.

When I got back about a hundred yards, I fled that place as fast as my feet would carry me. I never did see him, but he was there. I could smell him. Maybe the stiff breeze coming up that canyon covered my smell, or maybe it was a sweet smell of the lily of the valley, my savior, that covered my smell. Anyway, I thanked God all the way back to the quad. That was twice now in as many days, and I was paranoid about going anywhere.

A Harrowing Experience

I had accomplished a lot, but there was still a lot that needed to be done. I got more manure from the grotto and hauled it to my fields and spread it then tilled it in, then I dragged it over with my homemade harrow. I made the harrow out of a six-inch-thick cant twenty inches wide and eight feet long. I drove a row of ten-inch-long spikes through it in a row from one end to the other, another six inches behind that off set to the first row. This let them stick through about four inches. I pulled it all over my field, and it filled in the low places and made a beautiful little level field.

I planted a whole acre of corn. An acre is 208 by 208 feet. If you plant a stock every six inches, that's 416 stocks a row and at two foot intervals between rows, that's 104 rows even at one ear per stock. An acre has over forty thousand ears of corn and more. I planted the second acre into one third acre of wheat, one third of alfalfa, and the rest to that dark rye and barley and rutabagas and pumpkins. That's done, thank God.

Now I opened the back of the plane and retrieved the stuff I had stored there. I cleaned off the rest of the rock area. I had hot water from the spring under the potato bin and under the garden. I had a plug in the end. I had drilled little one-sixteen-inch holes about two feet apart in the one-and-a-half-inch pipe. This helped subirrigate the garden and heat the soil. Between this and the long summer days, you can't believe how fast that stuff grew.

I left the ATV parked where I could reach it by canoe to save time loading and unloading. My hope was to build a floating bridge from the natural ramp out around that outcrop of rock to the other side at a distance of about fifty feet, but I would have to have a knee in the middle with extra flotation. I first thought about big logs with extra floats under the center. This would also act as a dock on this side of the lake. If I put a small landing dock on the other side, I could go to the berry fields and also stockpile coal, peat, and pumice where it would be readily available summer and winter, all future plans.

The next day I went up to the coalfields where I also had found Liver Lips. I hoped to someday have a team of five or so moose to pack and pull and save on fuel. I killed a really old moose, whose bones popped with every step he took. I killed and butchered him for critter food and, yes, that tough old hide and tallow. His teeth were worn off clear to the gumline.

I went over to where I had picked strawberries. There were a lot of new plants emerging. I thought maybe if I picked through these and selected the most healthy ones and fertilized them, maybe I could get a bed of them that produced bigger berries. It was worth a try.

I went back over and loaded the moose quarters and headed home. I saw some nice fat yearling moose but would let them grow some more. Now I had some tallow to make three-wick candles to carry with me on the quad in case I got stranded. You never know what or where something might happen that you hadn't planned for, and it pays to be ready. I had a small insulated tent, a minus-forty sleeping bag, food for a week, and a little heat. I could survive.

MAKING SOAP

I had some lye going so I could make soap and/or hominy. If you soak corn in lye water, it will swell way up and turn white. Then you have to rinse it in fresh water several times, and you've got grits. To make the lye, I used one of the sixteen-gallon stainless steel pots and drilled one-sixteen-inch holes about an inch apart all over the bottom. Then I slid this down inside a twenty-gallon collection pot with spacers to hold it off the bottom for a place for the lye water to collect. I filled the sixteen-gallon pot with wood ashes and poured water over them.

As the water goes through the wood ashes, it extracts the lye out of them. You can use the lye water at this point, or you can evaporate out the water, and you have lye crystals that can be stored for the future. To reconstitute it, you simply add water back. I now had on hand enough crystals to last maybe ten years if need be.

Chance started to lick the water left in the bottom of my first soap batch and burned the tip of his tongue so badly, the skin came off about a half inch back. For a long time, he would yelp every time he tried to eat or drink.

I went to the upper valley and began clearing and leveling a place to relocate my sawmill to. I also made a place for another thirty-foot-by-forty-foot barn building. It was only about five hundred feet from the grotto, and I hoped it wouldn't disturb the sheep. They went up higher into the mountains in the summer when I would be doing most of my sawing, so I figured it would be okay. They would eat the emerging green grass in the spring then go higher into the mountains for the summer and fall.

The thousands upon thousands of grass clumps that grew up during the summer provided forage for the winter. The trees in the area were bigger with less tapper. They were higher quality in general. If I put four of the six railbed sections together, I could cut a forty-two-foot-long cant or plank. I would need long timbers and planks for the log house for the ceilings and floors.

A HIGHER PLACE

I had climbed that hill out in the middle of the valley several times. You could see past the valley walls from there in any direction. There was a flat place on top with one single tree growing out of it right in the middle. There was grass and muskeg growing up the side, but for the most part it, was just a big granite hill. Maybe it was the very top of a mountain at one time. Who knows? Long story short, I got some long poles about sixteen inches on the bottom, nine inches on top.

I climbed that center tree and hung the pulley block in it. I ran a cable from the foot of the hill clear to the pulley and back down to the bottom, hooked onto the top of the pole with one end of a cable and used Liver Lips and Samson to pull them up and set them in place. I had a ten-foot-by-ten-foot platform on top and a seventy-foot-high tower. A tree house if you will. I would put a little enclosed building on top of it later.

I made a stairwell and put a chair and a little stump for a table. I found myself singing as I worked. The name of the Lord is a high tower; the righteous run into it, and they are saved. I would go up there and glass the whole country side and also the valley floor. It was a sight to behold.

It was a great place to watch the northern lights from. Chance could go up or down my stairs okay. Bear got to the first landing and started back down. His front legs were too short, and he tumbled all the way to the bottom and broke my railing in the process.

TIME TO MAKE TURPENTINE

I drilled the centers out of a bunch of small branch pieces. I drilled holes through the middle longways and whittled down the end and then drove them into holes of the same size in the tree and hung a bucket on each to collect the spring sap that was running up the trees at this time every spring. This sap was like turpentine in consistency and smell.

I would get as much as a gallon a day from each tree and store it in some of my empty aluminum trunks. I had about ninety gallons in each one and would wind up with about twenty-five gallons of pitch tar. I would do this each spring and had about three hundred gallons of pitch tar stored for future use. I could use this for sealer, just like Noah did when he pitched the ark within and without.

I got my sawmill moved and set up. I cut a lot of trees and made lumber and cants in various dimensions and lengths. I cut a lot of long cants that could be timbers or planks or boards. I could always cut them into shorter lumber as needed. They were difficult to handle or haul, and I had to use the RTV and chain falls or come-alongs to get them on or off the cutting deck. A twelve-inch-by twelve-inch cant forty feet long is 480 board feet, and I could get four, maybe five of these a day, a day being seventeen or eighteen hours.

I found a smaller tree that had been broken over then started to go up again. It made a sort of tight S and was about five inches in diameter. I cut it out about eight feet long and saved it. I hope to make a new bed one day, and this would be the top of my headboard. There were a lot of trees, both small and big, that had these little deformities called burls. They were very decorative. I collected all of these that I found. If and when I would build a log house, I would use these for porch supports and other things inside and out.

I was always on the lookout for trees that had these on them. If I peeled the bark off the tree and branch that had these on them, I could then put the pitch that was just barely boiled down on them. It would preserve the color and add a sheen. I deduced I would use this on my logs also. It added a certain beauty and luster to whatever you used it on.

I set up one of the tents to store lumber in for now. I dug out some large plastic tarps to put over the mill. As soon as I got the barn built, I would store it there.

YE ARE THE SALT
OF THE EARTH

E very once in a while, I would get antsy to just go off somewhere and not have to concentrate on anything. When I
would scout, I would scout north to the high mountains and
west because it was above the tree line and open country, mostly just
moss full of blueberry plants with busted-up granite rock underneath.

I knew there was a lodge or settlement somewhere to the south
that the man whom I now knew the name of had told me about, but
how far? And it was all brush and scrub and would take one man
many years to cut through. And if you were off by even a few degrees,
you would miss it by miles. In this country where there is no density
of population, that's a disaster.

I went this day farther than I had ever been. The country started
to get more steep. There was a deep ravine I would have to go down
into and then a steep hill to get back out. I decided to try it today. If
I got over that hill, what would be on the other side?

Well, when I got over there, it wasn't nearly as steep as it had
looked to be. I was out maybe twenty miles and saw a barren area with
an alkaline-looking pool about in its center and lots of moose tracks
around it. I thought at first it was a moose wallow that was filled with
rainwater. I put my finger in it and then licked my finger—salt. Boy,
I could boil out the water and have lots of salt. I realized because of
the lack of vegetation, maybe all this area had salt in it.

I had a pick and shovel with me, so I got back about fifty feet
and dug off some overburden, and sure enough, it was just pure salt.
I cleared more area off and about a foot of top salt and had an area of
nice, clean white salt. I picked and scraped till I had two gunnysacks

about half full. That's about three hundred pounds per sack. It was all I could do to lift one into the back of the RTV.

I had a large tarp. I got some willow poles tied together and put the tarp over my cleaned out hole. I would be back for more shortly. I wanted to get a lot of it out and home before it could get soiled. I could run this through the pulverizer and have salt of any consistency. I would now have all the salt I would ever need for my table, for the critters. I could salt down hides till I had time to tan them. I could make pickles and cure meat. I could put eggs and vegetables down in it to preserve them. I could make ice cream. I could put it on the walkways to melt the snow. So many uses, and I now had all I could ever need. You are the salt of the earth. It made me wonder what all I was useful for.

I stopped by the strawberry patch and picked my hatful. It was midnight when I got back, and it was still light. I stored my berries in a little basket, covered them, and hit the hay. Tomorrow, I will make ice cream.

I had been very conservative with the salt I had because I didn't know how long I would be here, and our body needs salt, especially when you work hard and sweat it out of you. I got up early, did my daily chores, fed the critters that needed to be fed, gathered the eggs, made breakfast, and ate. Now I said, "Let's make some ice cream." I had salt, I had eggs, I had whole milk, I had sugar—everything that I needed.

I had a pail similar to a paint can; it had originally been used for syrup. It had a press-on lid and a wire bail. I had a tall ten-gallon stainless steel pot. I mixed up all the ingredients, even put some of that bummer lamb dry milk product in it and cooked it into a custard. I cooled then poured it into my gallon pail, allowing for the expansion of it freezing and room for the strawberries. I put a layer of ice on the bottom of a ten-gallon pot, then a handful of salt, then the pail, then ice, then salt, ice, salt, ice, salt till I had it to the top edge of the pail. I used the bail as a handle to turn it back and forth.

I would open it periodically and scrape down the sides of the pail and mix it in. When it was pretty thick, I put in the berries and mixed them in, closed the top, and let it set for about twenty minutes or so. Oh boy, my first ice cream in several years. I can't believe I ate the whole thing, but I did.

PIPE DREAMS

I was ready to finish the Pelton wheel project. I had the hot water already piped into the man cave and above the door and out to the creek's edge. The hot spring was actually about seventy feet higher than the intake to the Pelton wheel, but it had to travel horizontally the last fifty feet. I now divided the eight-inch pipe into four four-inch pipes and used two of them, which were divided into the intakes of the Pelton wheel. By dividing them this way, I could channel the rest to wherever I needed it at any given time.

I didn't know if I would have enough pressure to drive the four-KW setting or not. I got it all hooked up and started it up. It easily pulled four KW. Well, that's good and a relief.

I reconnected the ten-inch from the creek. I had tapped into it with a four-inch pipe and ran it all the way to the garden area along a ledge that ran about twenty-five feet over and then straight down. I hooked up a couple of garden hoses on the end of this. There seemed to be quite a bit of pressure in these one-inch hoses, and I could totally water the garden in about an hour a day.

Time was going by so fast, and I had a big workload. I had so much to get done while there was plenty of daylight. What if I got rescued? I would just have to pull up stakes and leave. So, God, please let me stay here until the snowfall at least.

GOLDEN OPPORTUNITY

I was now going to set things up so I could mine for my master. I had determined the yellow flecks in the sand really were gold. I had smelted some of it in my forge and made some ingots of about five pounds each. Where has all that come from? Then the light came on. Of course, that hot spring! Every time it blew, it spewed forth gold and sand. For eons, it had flowed out into the big house and settled out, then it had overflowed at some point and down my stairwell into the man cave area. About the time it got the man cave area filled to where it would go out into the creek, it had taken another course and ran out the way it was going now.

I had panned for gold quite a bit in my spare time, and I would get about fifteen ounces per pan. So in ten minutes, I could pan out about six thousand dollars' worth. That would amount to over twenty-five thousand dollars an hour. Why? There was no place to spend it, so why do it? I had a deep sense that it should be mined and stored for future use by somebody. I could stash it and keep a record of where I had stashed it.

There was that advanced model gold separator in one of the sheds across the lake. I read the manual. It had to have a water source and settling pond, but other than that, you only had to shovel in the gold-bearing sand, and it did the rest. I built everything for it, including the settling pond. I had packed in clay clear from the source on the far side of the upper valley and lined the dug-out pond area with it. The pond was twenty feet by twenty feet. I dug down a foot and a half and used that sand around the perimeter. I now had a pond three feet deep.

I put planks up the sides and on the bottom with a drain to go into the air intake tube. I would have to redo the air tube so the joints faced the other way so they wouldn't leak. I could also use this as an indoor swimming pool. I had noticed a small slit in the rock wall on my right facing in. Once in a while, there was a little puff of steam coming out of the top edge. Could there be another cavern behind that? Could the water running away from the hot spring be going out this direction? It was in the right proximity. Wherever that water was going, some force was also pulling the steam and vapor out that way too. If I was able to blow a hole in this wall into another cavern, would it push steam and vapor out or suck air back through?

I decided to take a chance; my curiosity got the best of me. I had run a piece of wire through that little top crack, and it hadn't hit anything on the other side. I made a perimeter of one-and-a-half-inch holes about six inches apart in a three-foot-by-six-foot-high area. I drilled clear through the first hole. It was only about eighteen inches. I knew there was space on the other side.

I planted the dynamite and let it bang. I had blown a three-foot-by-six-foot hole opening into a large cavern maybe thirty feet by forty feet and twelve feet to the ceiling. Sure enough, air was sucked in, not pushed out. How could that be? It went out through the same hole where the water went out. Was there a huge chimney flue where the hot air pulled the steam as it went? Would I ever figure it out?

The whole floor area of that cavern was just gold, chunks of gold, some nuggets as big as my fist, wire gold. There had to be billions upon billions of dollars here. I had found a mother lode. I was sure I was the richest man alive and had no way to spend it. I could have bought a trip to the moon, but I couldn't buy my way out of this spot I was in.

I built a wood door for the hole and got it sealed back up. I might get back to it this winter sometime maybe. The animals had all fled the scene. The chickens quit laying, and the bear had disappeared. My ears rang for three days, so the critters' ears probably did too. They had all huddled together in the far end and wouldn't eat or come for water.

HERE IN THE REAL WORLD

I had too much to do. I felt overwhelmed. I needed to get more blueberries and make more fruit leather and have dried berries for the birds. I needed to make more soap and candles, saw more lumber and get it packed up into the big house. I needed to stockpile more coal. I needed to build a dock on the other side of the lake. I needed to boil down more sap into pitch tar. I had nearly six hundred gallons of the turpentine stuff. The raw sap I stored in trunks. So much to do, so little time.

Sometimes I worked twenty hours a day. I would build up a so-called sleep debt and then sleep for a whole night and day. I made two tripods for fuel bladders. I pulled the bladders up with a chain fall and then put a platform for the bladder to rest on under it between the three legs and let the bladder back down to rest on the platform. Now I could fuel easier and in less time. I now had five empty fuel bladders, four of which were gas. I didn't have a plane wing with diesel fuel in it, so all five would be filled with gas out of the plane wing tank. How they had come through that crash without rupturing, I'll never know. Divine providence?

Now, how to get the gas out. I had a piece of one-inch rubber hose, but I couldn't suck hard enough on this to siphon. I fed a piece of fish tape through the hose and tied a wad of cloth soaked in hot tallow on the end. I got it down into the wing tank after working for a half hour getting the gas tank cap off. I pulled the fish tape through as fast as I could, and it siphoned. I got all five bladders full and back out from under the wing and up to the flat top. It all took less than two hours total. I had everything topped off and probably wouldn't have to do this again for maybe two years if I'm still here.

I got my dock over across done and ready to use. Now even after freeze-up, I could back a trailer under the edge of the dock and just shove it full. I had made two more trips with the RTV and trailer for salt and now had over two tons of it stored in my shed building. I decided to take enough time to go check on things in the upper valley.

I barged back over to my now grubbed-out trail that I had finished clear to my sawmill area. I called it my haul road. It saved me a lot of time and fuel as it took very little time for a round trip to the mill and back down. I would soon bring down more lumber and store it in the big house for winter projects. I planned to build a large, thirty-foot-by-forty-foot flat floor to work on in the big house between the light pole tripods.

Walking around in loose sand while trying to work is sometimes difficult. Having a good footing and a flat place to put things on or rest the work benches on. Well, it was a necessary plus. I got that done. The packing part, I did with the help of Samson and Liver Lips.

TIME TO RAMP UP

I had been looking at a little extended crevice at the far end of my field in the extended side valley. It was about twelve feet wide and narrowed as it went in and up. I got my long ladder that I had used to retrieve the big ram I had shot. I put it up at the far end of the split. There was a small ledge at that point about twelve feet across each way. It narrowed to about six feet and went to the left and angled up clear to the valley rim of the canyon. It came out close to where I found the pumice and lava beds. This could be easy access to all the north and west country and berry fields. Starting from this area I could save myself over twenty miles round trip.

I had planned to chisel out some large pieces of lava to use for foundation blocks for my house. You can cut lava with a wood chisel. I had made some large ones with a four-inch-wide blade using my forge and blacksmith know-how. I could cut a two-foot-by-three foot chunk of lava a foot thick in about an hour.

Now back to my original story. I stacked up a couple of logs crossways at the bottom end and laid the tops of four more on top of these. Then using pulleys and moose power, I pulled them up till the top rested on the lip of the ledge. The moose pulled while I pushed on the butts, and the lighter tops went up as they went in. They were all in place in one day without much difficulty. I cross planked them and had a ramp. Long story short, I drove the ATV all the way to the canyon top and back down.

America the Beautiful

I went back over to the sawmill to do some more cutting. On the way, I saw a cow moose that was skinny and limping. She wouldn't make it through the winter, so I did it for her. I butchered her and loaded the meat in the bed of the RTV. She would not have made it through the winter, and the bullet was a much easier way to go than starving to death. We went through eight or nine moose a year, half of it for Samson.

Just as I was leaving this place, I saw movement out of the left peripheral. I grabbed the .358 and then saw it plainly, a white head sticking up out of the grass, a bald eagle with a broken wing. I backed him into a brushy corner and threw my coat over him. That old boy was a symbol of our American heritage and freedom. I would save him if possible.

I turned around and started back, and it started to snow. I named him Yelp because that was all he did all the way back to the man cave. I'm sure he figured he was going to die. I took him into the cave and wrapped his whole body, except the broken wing, in fish tape. The big main wing bone was broken in two. It was a clean break that went through the bone at an angle for about two inches.

I trimmed off the wing feathers for a space of some four and a half inches Then I took some really small copper wire I had gotten from the windings of a small electric motor and put them around the bone about an inch or so apart. I snugged them down enough to hold the bone aligned then put a splint I had made from a round piece of limb with a half-inch hole I drilled through it longways. I put some tallow on a piece of light cloth and put that around the bone and the wood splint around that. I wired that together to form a splint. I wrapped the wing to his body and set him on the woodpile.

I got a piece of fresh meat from the kill and held it in front of him on a stick. He just stared at it for several minutes then grabbed it and gulped it down. I left more meat and a bucket of water in front of him and left a light on and went out. That evening, when I returned, the meat was gone and about a half inch of water. Maybe, just maybe, he would survive. He was so beautiful. Would our beautiful country that I love so much survive?

HARVEST TIME

I went up to the upper valley and harvested the wheat, the corn, and the barley. I had made a small threshing floor about four feet by four feet by four feet deep. I would lean down over the edge and beat a handful of sheaves of wheat or rye or barley against the side to get the grain off. It would hold all the wheat, so I would do it all, then I rigged a sifter in front of the reduced hole in the air shaft that blew air under the hopper spreader. I would dump grain into the hopper spreader, and it would trickle the grain into another container. So as the grain fell in front of the wind from the fresh air tube, it blew the lighter chaff away. A couple of times through, and the grain was completely clean. The chaff went to the birds; the wheat straw went for animal and bird nesting and bedding.

I shelled a lot of corn to be ground into cornmeal, partially what I fed to the moose and fully shucked the ones I would use for the pigs and chickens and turkeys. After they picked the cob clean, I gave the cobs to Liver Lips. I would build a fire in the evening in the big house, snack, and listen to hillbilly music and shuck corn. I could do seven or eight hundred ears in one evening. This year, I wound up with six hundred pounds of wheat, twelve pounds of barley, twelve pounds of dark rye, and thirty-seven thousand ears of corn I harvested and stored.

I dug the spuds, pulled and topped the rutabagas, and wrapped the cabbage I would be eating in cellophane. I sacked up the carrots, turnips, parsnips, and potatoes to go into the cooler. It took ten days to harvest and another forty of cleaning, grinding, shucking, and storing, but I got it all done. I tilled in the stubble, refertilized the wheat field, and replanted the hard Russian red wheat as it did better if it overwintered in the ground.

I got the rock pulverizer out and set it up with a ten-horse Kohler engine. The electric motor required 220 volts, and I didn't have 220. To grind, I simply put stuff under three inches in diameter into the top, and it came out the bottom flour. You could tighten the lower roller, which consisted of a bunch of round discs sandwiched together with little grooves in each. The more you tighten this, the finer ground the flour. I would finish the flour with my stone mill by hand.

I made salt in three different consistencies. I also had to clean it after each variety. I could remove the bottom roller and crush apples into a mush and catch it in a big pot. Then I had to press out the juice separately, but the crushing saved me a lot of time. When finished, I had milled two hundred pounds of fine flour from wheat, twelve pounds from barley, and twelve pounds from dark rye. I left about five pounds of barley whole to use for seed and my tasty pork barley and sauerkraut dish. I made eighty pounds of cornmeal, fifty pounds of fine salt, and six hundred pounds of granulated salt about one eighth of an inch in diameter.

I used the bigger stuff for animal salt, the same for hide preservation, for putting down eggs and vegetables. Tomatoes will stay fresh in salt for a year. You just take them out and soak them in fresh water overnight, then you have a better-tasting tomato than a store-bought one. I used it also for curing bacon, hams and briskets of moose, also for making pickles.

I also ground up all the bones and horns into bone meal. I would pick up and pack home all the caribou horns I found and bust them up and grind them. I had over one thousand pounds of bone meal.

Yelp was coming along just fine. He would take meat from my hand now. He had lost most of his fear of me. One day, it hit me. I had an orphanage going. A lot of them were from this native land. I felt we were as winterized as we would get. My critters would have plenty to eat. They had hay; they had alfalfa, corn, some wheat, spuds, carrots, cabbage, rutabagas, and pumpkins. Try finding that anywhere else in the world in the dead of winter.

I now had two sources of electric power—actually, three with the generators—a huge woodpile, and a coal pile. I had a farm, indoor housing, and a barnyard for my animals. It was complete with a large place to work and play. I had heat from the wood, coal, and/ or hot water. I had a good dry, warm place to live and plenty to eat. I was blessed beyond measure. I was happy and content but lonely, but I had Jesus—thank God for Jesus.

That woodpile took up nearly a quarter of my living space, but it was either that or pack it from the big house or from outside, so I opted for this. I was reminded of a story I once heard about a white man and an Indian man standing talking. The Indian said, "White man, we have really bad winter this year."

"Well," says Whitey, "how can you tell? Is it by the stars, by a sixth sense, by the wind? How do you know?"

"Me know because white man have big woodpile."

Well, I had a big woodpile and a big coal pile, that was for sure.

The Comforts of Home

My first project for this winter work would be a new and larger bed. I had that log with the S curve, some smaller pieces with the little burls. Some five inches down to two inches with burls for the lumber I used for the rest of the bed. I had redone and rearranged the mattresses so they were next to one another instead of on top of one another. I now have a bed seven feet wide and seven feet long. I guess that could be called a super king.

I made a pillow with a lambskin on one side and lynx catskin on the other and stuffed it with a chunked-up rubber mattress for filler. It was my pillow, the only one of its kind. I made a huge, nine-foot-by-nine-foot comforter four inches thick. I had lynx catskin squares sewed together for a top and the liner of a sleeping bag for the bottom. It was stuffed with duck down and sewed every six inches with some monofilament fishing line.

I made buttons out of moose horn tips to tie to hold it together. It was a beautiful masterpiece, at least I thought so. It hung past the foot of the bed over two feet and down each side about the same.

MY TROPHY ROOM

I had a lot of pelts, and that meant a lot of work. I developed a way to do the hard part, that of working the tanned skin till it was soft and pliable. Besides moose and sheep, I had forty grizzly bears, 130 wolves, two hundred lynx cats, forty wolverines, and a lot of beaver, muskrat, mink, and martin. I had them hung on poles that were buried in the sand of the big house. I had pegs all around the poles and the skins hanging from these. It was what I called my trophy poles.

Why do we have trophies? I guess it represents victories. All sports have trophies. When David killed Goliath, he cut off his head. That was a trophy. The churches of past times would hang crutches and wheelchairs on their walls. These were trophies of victories over diseases and sickness, reminders of healings.

I had once gone with a friend to a morgue freezer where the bodies of humans were laid out and kept in case someone could identify or claim them. There were bodies of runaway children, prostitutes, drug addicts, and murder victims. Then it hit me: this was Satan's trophy room.

The cross of Jesus is a trophy; it represents victory over death, hell, and the grave. Let us remind ourselves of that great event daily.

To work the skins after I had scraped all the fat off, I had made a perimeter of four-inch poles fastened on the corners then loose poles about four inches in diameter all across between the perimeter poles and pointing in the same direction all held within the twelve foot wide perimeter. I would tack down the edges of skins to these poles and then drive the ATV or RTV over them till they became soft and pliable.

Because of the poles' moving and turning, they were stretching the skins. This would take about fifteen minutes to finish a cured and tanned hide. I could stretch and roll two grizzly or moose hides at one time or several of the smaller animals. This all was done in the dry summer months because the thing had to be on the flat rock surface. I didn't kill any caribou because I didn't care for the taste of their meat.

MY ROCK

I then moved my entire operation up into the big house for the winter. I had wondered many times what I would have done. Where would I now be if it weren't for this rock, especially if it wasn't for the cleft in the rock? This cave, could I have survived without it? My God—my all-powerful, ever-present, all-knowing God—had formed this place eons ago. He knew that someday, I would come here. Had he done this just for me? Is he that personal? If I had been the only human ever made, would he have done it just for me? Would he have loved me that much?

This place, carved out of the solid rock by just one word, preserved and reserved until the time was right. This solid place, my sanctuary, my covering, my fortress, a place of warmth and protection in a harsh environment. This shelter, this hiding place, my security, my place of prayer and worship, a source of cool clear water, a spring giving forth life abundantly, my very salvation. It has always been. Rock of ages, cleft for me a place of fellowship, a place of work and rest, a place of unfathomable riches—my rock.

GOD IS FAITHFUL

I pulled the outside intake to the Pelton wheel and hooked up the hot spring water to it. I was a little skeptical that the hot water might warp it. It was really heavy cast alloy; the generator itself was separate with a shield between the housing for the wheel and the working parts of the whole thing, the wiring, and so forth. After three days, I relaxed; it was fine.

I had to rearrange that gutter from the outside creek edge, clear up into the big house. I had to knock out a partition of lava rock that was between the edge of the big house and the top of the stairwell so water would not have to go over a hump to run down, also so I could drain the settling pond. The lava rock drilled easily, and I made several holes about four inches apart then used a sledgehammer to bust it out.

Without the fresh air the big house felt stuffy, and it was too warm for the animals with their winter coats of hair. It was too warm for me when working hard, but it freshened the air and carried off the smells. That hot spring erupted every eighty-seven days faithfully, and each time, it dumped more gold and sand particles. The heavier gold would land first, then the sand would be washed off and away down the tube. It was a natural separator, if you will. I and the critters had gotten used to it, but it was still unnerving every time it happened.

I took the splint off Yelp's wing. He could get around pretty good, sort of jump-fly up onto tables or shelves or my arm. The wing feathers were showing but hadn't grown back to where he could totally fly.

I kept a grow light on for about seventeen hours a day, and this had enough light to shatter the darkness clear over to the animal pens. The eyes adjust to only this much light, and it appears almost daylight.

I had taken Ovinia up and turned her loose in the upper valley, hoping she would get pregnant. She would sometimes disappear for several days at a time. Sometimes I could holler for her, and she would show up. I was pretty sure I had killed all the grizzlies, but I was worried something might have killed her. But then when the air turned and took on that certain chill feeling and the winter winds were starting to set in, she followed me home one day, even got on the barge without my coaxing her. She was so loving; all the critters were. They seemed to develop a comradeship between them and between them and me. We had to depend upon one another. It was a survival instinct. They would sometimes romp and play together.

My little sow pig, "Sour," was getting fat. She was young, but I soon realized she was going to give birth. Well, she had fifteen little piglets. What does one man do with fifteen little pigs? I ate the first one when it weighed about fifteen pounds—killed it, scalded it, scraped off the hair, gutted it, and stuffed it with a sage bread stuffing. I put an apple in its mouth and roasted it over an open fire. Maybe later, I would turn some loose in the upper valley to see if they could survive. For now, I would just keep my Wilbur the bore pinned up separately. But now I have a start. I could have all the baby back ribs, bacon, hams, pickled pig's feet, headcheese, lard, etc. that I could eat.

Samson had really gentled down. I doubt he was capable of knowing why. I called him my big live teddy bear. I made a harness and pack bag for him. Now I would have to get him used to them and train him to work, to obey my wants and needs. He needed to earn his keep; after all, the chickens gave back in eggs and meat, the turkeys would also by next year, the pigs in meat and lard, the moose in work. I could trap the ducks and pluck down off their breasts. I had twelve gunnysacks stuffed with it. Chance was a close companion and a warning system. Yelp, well, he was pretty to look at and reminded me of my freedom.

I kept two hens and a rooster from the last hatch. My older hens were laying well right now. I was putting eggs down in salt for future use when they would be in a molt slump and not laying well. I saved all the fat from the chickens I butchered. Chicken fat is the only fat that will stay fluid when cold. I would render it, screen it till it was like a fine oil, and use it for gun oil. Last year's old hens were fast asleep in the freezer. They would make good chicken and dumplings or chicken and noodles. They had all done their part. Faithful is as faithful does.

FORT KNOX

I had reclosed the hole I had blown into what I now called Fort Knox with a huge wooden door. Now I opened it. It was too hot to stand in front of. I made a long handle rake and reached in and twisted some of the wire gold into the tines. I could see there were billions upon billions of dollars here. I was rich beyond my ability to grasp it all, but why? It would take special equipment to retrieve it, and I didn't have special equipment. I had found what prospectors refer to as the mother lode, the very source of where all the other gold had originated, the bounty of Mother Earth.

Then a revelation hit me. All this that had happened had been allowed by God for a purpose in my life. All the mental strain, all the hurt, all the loneliness, the heartaches, the long nights laboring in prayer, the heartbreak, the trying desperately to sort things out—I found it. I had finally found all that I had been searching for, something so precious, it was indescribable. I had found the father lode, the source of all things present, of all things powerful, of all things that are known and unknown, all things spiritual and eternal—the father lode. He will someday make me heir with his Son, the very thing that many seek but few find. This experience had changed me, redirected my goals, changed my thinking, I was in this world but not of this world.

When I had blown the hole in the wall, the animals had all tried to hide. Chance avoided me. On the fourth day, I heard something above me. I looked up and there was Samson nestled between the three tops of the tripod for the lighting. I spoke to him gently, and he came speeding down backward and headed straight for the water tank. Chance saw all this and came over, wagging his whole body.

I celebrated by taking the day off. I made a large stew. I made cinnamon rolls. I made ice cream. I just relaxed and spent time with my critters. Actually, I think I was trying to regain their confidence.

There seemed to always be a part of me that said you need to get things done. I always loved to work and to accomplish things. Now I wanted to get that hot water radiator going. It presented a challenge to me. If I put it high enough, I could come off the bottom exhaust manifold then back up about four feet then across about ten feet and down to my tub and wash area. This would leave me ample room below for my critters or the RTV, for that matter, to go past and under and up.

I used Samson about every day now to pull and pack for me. He would go up and down the stairwell with a full load all the way to the freezer. He could pull eight hundred pounds up that stairwell with ease. He acted like he never even knew he was pulling anything. Then I would give him a half dozen Skittles, and he was ready to do it all again. He was strong as a bear.

I got the heater all plumbed in and working. It kept the man cave warm even without the wood stove, but it lacked that dry, cozy feeling. I would build a wood fire every evening and watch a movie and eat popcorn. It was really a good life but oh so lonely. I would think of my sweetheart every day and wondered if she ever thought of me. There is no pain quite like loving someone so much and not being able to be with them.

A NEW SPORT

*When a new color, blossom or size differs from the
mother plant, this is referred to as a sport.*

I had a large tomato plant starting to bloom. This one was a hybrid, a sort of cross between a determinant and a nondeterminant. It was a bush that had to be caged as it grew to about four feet tall and two feet wide. It had huge tomatoes that had good flavor. Unlike most determinants, it kept on setting more fruit as it grew and aged. Some of these will produce for four months under grow lights. The first tomatoes would be ripe by fifty days from seed. If I kept the seed cool, it would last maybe twenty years.

I also had a gazebo cabbage that, in this country, would reach sixty pounds. I also had quart-size canisters of that seed and kept it cool. I wasn't sure how long it would last. I grew about three hundred of these a year. It made for a good green feed for the critters. I had made several four-foot-square-by-three-foot-deep wood containers for the cool room and more for the cold room. I had to expand the freezer area another twenty feet just to hold all the vegetables and meat. I couldn't turn water into wine, but I could turn moose poop into vegetables and a bullet into a fine steak.

I was looking at my strawberry bed one day when I noticed a runner with a new and darker leaf and a still white berry about one inch in diameter. The end of the runner rooted in and made a new plant. I air layered the runner in several places along it, hoping it would root and form more like plants. If they root, a new plant will start at that point, and after it roots in well, you clip it loose and plant it separately, and then in time, when they send out more runners, you can repeat the process. By midsummer of the next year, I had over four hundred new large strawberry plants. They all have that terrific wild strawberry flavor.

THE LIFE OF RILEY

I had things to keep me busy but nothing pressing. It was mostly just maintenance now. I was relaxed and not too concerned as at first. It was a good feeling, or God forbid, was I starting to get old?

It was getting really cold out now, forty or fifty below. I didn't go outside much. I brought the RTV up into the big house for the winter just to store it and used it once in a great while just to start it and run it some. I felt it needed that. I didn't like the chore of getting dressed up warmly for only a little while, and I got all the exercise I needed and then some anyway. I would turn off the main lights twelve hours a day just to create a day-and-night effect.

I funneled air through my air tube gutter and shut it off enough to maintain about sixty degrees in the big house. I decided to channel that cold air into Fort Knox to see if I could cool it down enough to be able to go in there. I let it cool for two days and then tried it. I put my hand in slowly; it felt normal. I put my whole bare arm in, and it still felt normal. I threw in a couple of planks to walk in on and a couple of stainless steel buckets and stepped in. It was almost too cool at that floor level. Warm air goes up, cold down.

I started looking around Fort Knox. There was a five-foot lava tube on the far left lower corner facing in, and right above that was a two-foot hole in the ceiling area. I got over there, and I could see the vapor being sucked into that hole. No wonder it didn't go out into the big house. If that wasn't there, it would have sucked it back through the big house, and it would have been much warmer, and condensed air would have given the big house a rainy-like atmosphere.

I filled a bucket with gold and couldn't lift it. I filled it halfway and could get it out the doorway. I dumped it just to the right of said doorway. I got out what I guessed would be about three thousand pounds that day, probably about thirty-five million dollars' worth. Not bad for one man in one day. But why? What was it worth to me? A lot of work and nowhere to spend it.

I knew that the fifty-foot-high wall was warm to the feel, but now I put a thermometer against it and covered it. There were 120 degrees coming off that wall.

RETURN TO NORMAL

I started making gallon-size wooden pots with one-inch thick wood I had split out. I could have plants that had blooms on them when I set them out and tomatoes to eat thirty days later in the greenhouse garden.

I was hammering away, and something hit my shoulder and screamed in my ear. No, my wife hadn't found me. My hair stood on end, and I got goose bumps on top of goose bumps all over. I knew instantly what it was, but it still scared the wits clear out of me. Yelp had decided to pay me a little friendly visit. I would turn him loose this spring. I knew Ovinia had a kid in her, but I didn't think Liver Lips did, although she was probably old enough now. I had made a hackamore for her; that's a bridle without a mouth bit.

I also made a saddle of sorts and some pack bags. The saddle was fashioned after the army pack saddle with a cross of wood that stuck up about four inches on either side of the front and back cantles to hang pack straps over. I made a heavy pad for a seat for myself and a saddle blanket made of lambskin fleece side down. I put a hundred-pound sack of potatoes on her and led her around the big house. She actually seemed to like it.

When I finally decided to ride her, she took to it right away. I had ridden bronc when I was a kid on the ranch in Nebraska and figured if she bucked me off, I would have soft sand to land on. I did stop to think and wonder if she was mad enough to buck me off, would she turn around and stomp me to death? She never tried to buck, and after that, I rode her around the big house almost daily. It was good for both of us.

I had a chance to get a baby arctic fox one time and also a pair of baby caribou calves. I thought about it but decided I didn't need a fox in my chicken house or caribou that I didn't really like.

I Need a Bridge

I need a bridge, a go-between. I drew up plans for a floating bridge from my ramp and around the outcrop of rock. I didn't know if I would have enough flotation right in the center where the logs from each side would meet. I thought about fuel bladders for floats, but I would need them. "Well," I said to the only man around to talk to, "why not make some out of lumber?"

I would need eleven to space them on four-foot centers. I made fourteen. I used three-by-twenty-inch lumber ten feet long. I cross braced them corner to corner at three intervals on the inside and extra in corners and side corners. I heavily coated them inside and out and a lot extra in the seams with pitch tar. I decided to use six-inch poles across the tops longways spaced one foot apart instead of big logs as my first plan. I would put a handrail along the inside edge. The outside edge I would leave open so I could use it as a dock. That bridge would hold up a small tank if need be.

I figured I had now pulled over thirty tons of gold from Fort Knox. I would always work so hard and get so tired out and then ask myself why. But there was something inside of me that seemed to be saying that someday, it would be needed. Why else would it even be there?

I wanted to get out more while the cold arctic air cooled Fort Knox down enough. Little did I know that by the time it would be used, it would be worth four times as much as it now is. I needed to get it outside and put it somewhere in case of an earthquake and the whole mountain came down. I loaded gold on Liver Lips and made five trips a day to the stash that was a couple hundred feet down the outlet creek. I could haul more on the RTV, but I wouldn't be able to go all the way from the gold stash pile to where I dumped it.

I would only put three hundred pounds on Liver Lips at a time, as she had a little trouble going down the stairwell. I had put some cross pieces about every foot so her feet could brace against them, and she could go up it with five hundred pounds or more, but going down her front feet would tend to slide, and it made her nervous. I had drawstrings on the bottom of the pack bag so it emptied fast. We would get out about 1,500 pounds in three hours, and that was enough for both of us. It still left me enough time to do other things. Liver Lips's body wasn't used to the cold air, and she would want to run back, but I usually rode her back, so I kept her to a fast walk.

I got all the gold out in six weeks and threw some brush over it. I yearned for spring to come with its daylight and warmer air and new life in everything. I had a book of *The Works of Flavius Josephus to Which Are Added Seven Dissertations Concerning Jesus Christ, John the Baptist, James the Just, God's Command to Abraham, Etc by Flavius Josephus* by Josephus the Jewish historian. There was a lot in that book that corroborated what the Bible says even though he disputed Moses's writings quite a bit. I would read it just for the history. In one place, it talks about Abraham as he went out to follow God. He had amassed huge herds of camels, sheep, goats, and donkeys. They were nomadic because of the amount of graze it took for so many animals.

The custom of the time was that if you dug a well, you owned the grazing rights to that territory. Abraham dug wells and made altars of sacrifice to God and worship places. He would pile up a pile of rocks, put a pole down in the center with a red flag on top that could be seen from far off. It meant he held claim to that territory. Jesus put a pole down in a pile of rocks called Golgotha and, thereby, laid claim to the souls of men of the past, present, and those that are far off.

Another story I liked was about David. When he killed Goliath, Jewish history says he cut off his head and packed it all the way to what is now Jerusalem and hung it on a pole—thus, the place of the skull. I thought that was interesting.

NEW LIFE

S pring finally came; the sun came out again. The days got longer and longer. The birds began to sing, and I have been here
just under three years. New life comes every spring, and there
was new life in my camp: a new baby ovine ram and a new baby
bull moose. A moose is of the deer family, so you can't really call it
a bovine. I named the new baby ovine Rambo and the moose baby
Blabbermouth.

Well, it was time to stop playing and get busy again—all the
ground prep, the planting, the replenishing, the building. I had to
cut more lumber. I had started a floor in the man cave but had to
stop because I ran out of lumber.

I went to the upper valley and tilled and replanted the rest of
the grain. The alfalfa was ready to cut for the first time. I would likely
get four cuttings off it this year. I got an area ready and planted my
cole crops, most of which were cabbage. I also planted rutabagas,
squash and pumpkins. Just those four items produced over thirty
thousand pounds, most of which would be animal food.

I now had a source of milk, both sheep and moose. Ever milk
a moose? The first time I tried to milk her, she turned her face way
back toward me and laid back her ears. She raised her hind leg like
she wanted to kick me. I spoke to her gently, and she backed off and
quieted down.

BULLWINKLE

Sometime later, she followed me to the upper valley. Blabbermouth was with her. I had the saddle and hackamore in the bed of the RTV. I decided to go moose back riding. I put on the hackamore and saddle and climbed aboard. I was looking at little Blabbermouth. That little gangly, long-legged thing, how could anything be so ugly and yet so cute?

Liver Lips started prancing around and wanted to get going. She was loving this. We got clear over in the southeast corner, and Liver Lips took off so fast that she almost unseated me. She was in panic mode, running full out, with Blabbermouth nearly underneath her and trying to keep up.

I got my head turned back, and the biggest bull I had ever seen was only about five feet behind. Thank God I had the .44 Redhawk in my belt. I hauled it out and pointed it back in (what I hoped was) the right direction and dropped the hammer. Liver Lips stopped so fast, I went flying over her head and piled up. It was like everything went into slow motion. I rolled over and over and over and stopped with the .44 pointed back. That bull was upside down, hind legs still kicking. I tried to stand up, but my legs were like rubber. Was I hurt?

I started to shiver and shake, and it seemed like an hour before I could stand. Both moose were just grazing away, perfectly content. I'm six feet four inches fingertip to fingertip. With my left fingers on his right horn facing me, my right fingers still had twenty some inches to the outside edge of his left horn. That bull then was over ninety inches wide, hornwise. This no doubt was the same bull I had seen two years ago when glassing the valley.

I rode Liver Lips back to the RTV unsaddled and turned her loose. I went back with the RTV and butchered the bull. I slipped the brains out through the cerebral cavity. I bleached the skull white and made what is called a German mount and hung that rack in my man cave. I called it my bullwinkle mount.

I cut a pile of planks to finish my man cave floor and also the floating bridge. I had put some planks longways clear across to walk on. Now I would take these off and cross plank the six-inch poles so I could drive across. I braided several lengths of galvanized cable together into a cable to hang the center of the bridge off the wall above. I anchored it in several places to rebar. I had driven into cracks in the wall. Then I put the biggest chain fall I had and connected it to all this to lift the center of the bridge a little to help support it. It would also be able to lift it clear out of the water so the ice couldn't crush my floats in the winter. That chain fall was slow, but it was rated at twenty-five tons. It took twenty minutes to raise the bridge center three inches.

I harvested forty-five thousand ears of corn that fall, and the wheat gave me eight one-hundred-pound sacks of grain. I would wait till the winter to finish my man cave floor. I put a partition wall between my living area and the woodpile. I would put shelves across the front of it to put things where I could find them easier. I plan to build a chest of drawers and put it on the stairwell end of that wall and the mirror up above. All this would fit up against the room side of the partition.

HOW THAT ROOM
WAS ARRANGED

S tarting at the back wood wall, which was twenty-six feet from the front and nineteen feet wide after I had removed the two more feet of sand, there was a two-foot space from the edge of the shelves to the edge of the stove then six more feet of space to the front edge of my couch facing toward the stove. My big chair was to the left end of the couch and also faced the stove and it's left side toward the front of the chest of drawers.

Behind the couch, with one side against the back of the couch, was my seven-by-seven-foot bed. Then a couple of feet, and I had a small table and folding chair. Two more feet and the window area and my winter fridge freezer. There were eleven feet between the end of my couch and the back of the chair to the straight up wall. The tub stuck four feet out into the eleven but still left seven feet wide and that still left enough room for the RTV or the pack animals when they were fully loaded.

I had some cupboards above the tub, which opened from either side and some more under the fridge area for my eating utensils, my bowls, trays, salt and pepper, and spices.

A Necessary Toy

O f all the toys of men, a wife is the most expensive but also the most necessary and most desired. Another necessary toy: a snowmobile of sorts. The wheels and tires of the carts were all the same as the ones on the ATV. I'm sure they were designed that way on purpose, a lot of spares if needed. I wanted the back drive wheels to be twice as wide or dually for a lot more surface.

I sandwiched two together by cutting round pieces of log about the right diameter. Then I cleaned them up so they slid inside the wheels. To do this, I had to put the outside tires on backward. After switching these around to match the other ones, I put all thread bolts clear through one wheel to the other that ran through the wood also and pulled it all tightly together. I could disengage the front wheels so they would still pivot but no power to them.

Then I built a pair of six-inch-wide, six-foot-long skis that were shaped on the bottom like any ski. I forged a piece of one-eighth-inch-thick steel runners on their face. I cut a place to drop the front wheel into and strap them in with ratchet straps. The front rode a little high, but this thing went over snow like a real snowmobile. I had to hold back playing on it because I didn't want to waste fuel. I could now go from the flat rock to the falls area of the valley in less than ten minutes.

THE LOG HOUSE

I had put a log house together in my mind and revised it mentally about a hundred times. I had it well designed, but I would draw it and redraw it until I was satisfied with it. I got started on it in the fifth year. I cut a lot of the right-size trees, cataloged them, put down some sacrifice logs. and laid the logs I would use across these to dry. They would dry for the summer and then they would freeze dry in the winter and be ready to use the next spring.

I chiseled out thirty-six two-foot-wide-by-three-foot-long and a foot-thick large piece of lava stone to use for the foundation. It is easy to cut; it is strong and stays together well. I had these spaced around the perimeter and at intervals throughout the center area. I laid down a perimeter of eight-by-twelve squared timbers and crossed the center with the same. Then I laid a three-inch-thick floor on these then a row of logs on that and a second floor that was three inches thick also. I used thick boards and an air space between to give an insulation effect.

I had left a place on one end open to the ground to put the fireplace on. The base for the chimney was a huge chunk of lava. I had made channels for air between the two floors, two low channels and two high channels and a place in the middle above the first floor to put the heat radiator in. It would lie flat at a slight angle, offset by four inches. The hot water would come into the top end manifold and go out the bottom exhaust manifold and then on out.

I stopped building for that year. When finished, I would have a house that was one story on the back and two stories on the front. It would have a fourteen-by-forty-foot porch upper and lower. It would have a triple roof counting the barn shakes. It would face south with the big hot pool behind it up against the wall, the small lake and

132

waterfall on the left. It was a little higher than the foundation of the house and had been carved out of solid rock by the eons of time. Both of the upper and lower porches had burl poles for support; they were eight feet apart. It was stunning to look at.

The hot spring above the pool came out of a wall about thirty feet up. I made a trough out of eighteen-inch-wide and twelve-inches-deep planks that went partly out into the hot water coming out of the wall and carried it down to the little lake, then another one from the little lake back over to the hot pool. This circulated cold water to cool the pool, and my hope was it would cause some of the lake to stay open all winter.

I also ran a six-inch pipe from the hot spring down and underground to my radiator heat source, and it exited into a little pool about sixty feet in front of the house. I had dug this pool and lined it with clay. I was pretty sure it would stay open, but there would be a huge overflow that would freeze as it ran over and out into the creek bottom.

There were a lot of ducks, turkeys, and pigs, along with about sixty moose in the valley on the mountain now. I had counted seventeen bull moose with over eighty-inch racks. Bullwinkle's gene pool was still here. I now have five moose that would pull or pack. Liver Lips had had triplet bulls in her fourth year, all of them were fixed so they wouldn't be fighting or interested in the cows. They would get a little ornery sometimes. Besides Liver Lips, there was Blabbermouth, Rubber Nose, Snot Nose, and Ug-lee.

BACK TO THE HOUSE: YEAR 6

I made a huge rock fireplace from lava rock and cemented it together. I knew how to make a little scoop shelf in the back of the bottom of the chimney. This scoop caused the air going up the chimney to draw new air down the chimney on the back side and send it back up. This prevented the smoke from coming out into the house on a windy day. Whoever invented that idea had his head screwed on right.

I had used Samson, Liver Lips, and Blabbermouth to get the logs rolled up on the walls. Bear would work for a few skittles and the moose for peanuts, literally.

I put in plexiglass windows with double panes. I used some one-inch round stock between the panes to make it look like it had twenty-four single panes in one window. I made a lava rock barbecue pit in the center of the lower porch and a dome-shaped brick oven on one corner. I made the brick out of clay. I had made some reusable wooden molds. I pressed the mixed and kneaded clay into them, dumped them out, and let them sun dry. Then I piled them up in a circle, put a piece of metal over the top, and built a fire inside and let them bake into brick. I then mortared them together in a dome shape with a little chimney. I would build a small fire on one side and bake bread or do a roast on the other. Between it and the barbecue pit, I could do a whole meal outside.

I boiled down some pitch to a still thin consistency and painted the whole house with it. It helps preserve the logs and gives them a shiny amber-colored sheen. I made a lot of bear rugs. The biggest and best was the one I made out of two skins, one on top and another on the bottom, then stuffed in between with some thinner-cut rubber mattress. I left the head on the upper side. It was unique to say the least. I had taken pitch tar and mixed sawdust in it.

I would take a bear skull. I boiled the meat off the head then screwed the jaws together and then replaced where the meat had been with the sawdust tar mixture. I would let this dry for a couple of months then shave or file it till it had a natural bear head shape, put the skin part over it, and I had a very natural-looking head on a bearskin rug. I had two of these plus the double one on my living room floor and one in each of the upstairs bunk rooms. I put that moose head over the fireplace and some sheep horns and caribou horns I found.

I made two chandeliers out of moose horns. I used a bunch of single one-side sheds (shed horns). I made metal plates sixteen inches in diameter. I heated them and bent them into very shallow bowls. I drilled through the centers to run the light cords through. I put a ceramic light base on each. I had several fluorescent circle lights that would screw in like a regular light bulb. They put out the equivalent of two hundred watts. I bolted the base of each horn to the metal so the antlers were all around with insides facing down. This made a huge bowl-shaped chandelier. I hung the two of these from the top ceiling log about ten feet apart.

I had the house pretty much decorated for a man. I intended on spending my time up here for four months a year now. I had it all finished and moved into the summer of the ninth year. I would sit on the upper porch and watch the ducks and turkeys and pigs. The wild critters would come around also: arctic fox, lynx cats, and wolverines. I would see marten and mink a lot, and the moose would come and lie down next to the warm pond. About half of the pond would stay open all year.

I never did see a grizzly or any tracks or scat, so I was pretty sure I had cleaned them all out. But then again, I thought I had them all before the encounter when Samson had killed that one and saved my life.

The beaver tried to build a little dam across the lower end. That would have backed the water up where I didn't want it. So I would tear out the dam, then they would build it back time and again. I finally got tired of this and trapped them out. The lynx and fox would kill the ducks and turkeys and even the baby pigs, so that kept them pretty well in control. I harvested what I needed. If and when I needed, I would trap out the lynx and fox. This was the reason I had so many tanned skins.

I kill wolves whenever I have the opportunity. Wolves are vicious animals. They kill just for the sport of it. I have found young moose and caribou that they had brought down. They would eat the rectum area out of the animal when it was still alive and leave it there to suffer, sometimes for days, before it died.

MY BARBECUE SPIT

I put a paddle wheel at the lower end of the descending water trough. I ran a stainless steel cable through a half-inch stainless steel pipe and attached it to both the paddle wheel on one end and the spit on the other. The water power would slowly turn my roast over the fire. The hot water going into the lake would keep the edge of the lake open in turn, and it circulated cold water back into my hot pool. It kept it cool enough, I could swim in it year-round, even go swimming on purpose when it was forty below. I would build a fire next to the pool to undress and redress by.

Yelp would bring me snowshoe rabbits or a duckling or a young turkey or baby pig almost weekly. He would then fly up on the porch banister and sit and watch. I would act like I was eating it raw. It was our little thing. I guess it was his way of paying me back. He had found a mate, and they had built a big nest in the top of a fir tree about two hundred yards west of my house. I would use the binoculars to watch them from the time they hatched till they grew enough to leave the nest.

I had put a little house on the tree house platform. I would go over there sometimes and glass the whole area and stay the night and watch the northern lights.

MY ORCHARDS

I saved the seed from Jonathan and King apples, vernalized them, and planted the seeds. Pretty close to everyone grew. I kept them for two years and planted them out when they were about four feet tall. I planted several in the end of the area where my fields were. I took the rest clear over to the northeast end and planted them along that wall. In all, I had sixty-three trees.

I had also planted some walnut trees. I had acquired these by planting store-bought walnuts. I didn't think they would grow, but they did. I kept a hive of bees in each area. Because of late frost, I would get lots of apples some years and then some not.

I had a fence across the canyon where the fields were, but none for those on the northeast wall. They had a wall behind them, so I simply put a twelve-foot-high split-rail fence across the front of them. The moose would not only eat the apples, but they would destroy the tree also.

I had made a lot of square wooden barrels about two feet by two feet square by three feet deep. They would hold about eighty gallons of liquid. I had them cinched tight top and bottom with cable. When the wood soaked up, they wouldn't leak.

I kept about a hundred pounds of apples for pie and fresh eating then fill a couple of barrels with apple juice for cider. I would let it ferment just till it started to get a little bite to it. Then I would put it up in gallon-size Ziploc bags and freeze it. I would have hot or cold cider all year long this way.

One year, I realized I would run out of vinegar. I left one barrel to ferment clear out. I had a couple of gallon jugs that had vinegar with the mothers still in them. I put these in that barrel and closed it up. Six months later, I opened it. I had the best unwatered-down vinegar I had ever tasted. I used it for many things: for pickling, for cleaning. If I made a kill, I would wash it down with vinegar to keep the blowflies off and help tenderize the meat. I would take a spoonful a day for my health.

I had a good life here. I was content even if I was lonely. The Bible declares that godliness with contentment is great gain.

What I Didn't Know

M y family had nearly gone bankrupt trying to find me. The main search had been ten miles to the south. One plane had actually flown over where I was, but the recent snow had covered the skid marks of the crash, and I was still unconscious at that point. The plane was also covered with snow and tucked into the neck of the creek bed pretty much out of sight from the air. If there ever was a crash indicator on that old military plane, it had quit working long ago.

Fred had gotten the pilot to swerve north to look at the valley on the mountain, as he called it. The port engine had shut down, and one engine couldn't pull the load he was carrying, and we had gone down. Tony was now sole heir to Fred's fortune: nearly ninety million dollars and all the land and building projects. The government, bless their little hearts, had taken nearly half of the ninety million.

Tony had married and moved north to try to build on Fred's dream. He had finished the lodge and added more rooms. He had built a lot of new log houses all around the lake, some for family members who wanted to be a part of it, some for permanent workers, and some for special needs like a pastor and a doctor and a nurse.

There were six more lakes in the descending valley where the big lake emptied back out. Two of these were on his property, four were on tribal lands. Tony had arranged a fifty-year renewable lease on these and built houses and lodges on each. These lakes were small, twenty to thirty-five acres. Every place was run off diesel generators that he had brought in for power. Several families would book ahead several years, and this would be like a vacation or extended vacation.

Because some would stay several weeks or even months, the lodges would sleep up to twenty-five people each. There were two families who leased the lower last lake every year from mid-October to mid-March. One family had eighteen members and lived in the lodge. The other had twelve and lived in a large log house. They would ice fish, ice-skate, snowmobile, ski, and have parties on the ice. They did a hunt for moose and caribou. There was even an open sidehill that they could light up and ski on. They were pretty much on their own most of the time, and I guess you could call it their winter home.

Back at the main lodge, it was always hustle and bustle. Tony was able to use the hot spring extensively to heat the main lodge and some of the closer houses. He had made a large swimming pool that was built in such a way as to look natural. He also had a smaller indoor one. He had redone the runway to accommodate two Learjets and commercial and cargo planes also. He now had six Beaver and three Kodiak for sightseeing trips. It was a huge operation.

Fred would have been thankful and happy. My three daughters all wanted to be a part of it. I had a whole parcel of grandkids I had never met or even knew I had. Each person, including Tony, had a salary that amounted to twice what they could make in the lower forty-eight. They all ate together at the lodge. This was used to pray over and coordinate the day.

Tony's wife had started a side business, a little day care center. People could leave their children and know they were well cared for. They all owned their own home on lakeside property. There was a promise of a bonus if the place ever got to where it was making money. The property had an arrangement in a co-op setting, so if they ever wanted to not be there any longer, they had to sell to the co-op or another blood relative.

My oldest daughter was in charge of all the accommodations and making the guests comfortable and content. Her husband was gifted in construction design and oversaw all new construction. My second daughter was a renowned cook and had charge over foods and dining and a huge bank of chefs. Her husband was over all the hunting and fishing, the guides, the snowmobile trips, outpost hunts, and so forth. He also was a bush pilot and was over the other bush pilot activities. My third daughter and her husband both flew the jets to bring in the guests from Anchorage and then take them back. She also brought in the mail.

It was a smooth-running operation with four hundred guests a week and was booked ahead two years. They charged one thousand dollars a week per person, which included travel to and from Anchorage, lodging, food, sports, parties, fishing, ice-skating, field trips, hiking, trail rides on four wheelers in summer or snowmobiles in winter, dogsled rides, and more. Outpost hunting and fishing trips with guides were more, and flying into other areas were more.

There was a deposit to be held to cover things like vandalism, theft, and so forth that was refundable when they left. They could leave at any time if they wanted, but their stay charge and flying were not refundable. They had to fly out on their own dime. If strict rules were broken, they were expelled and sent out. There was no alcohol or drugs. If they were caught, they were escorted back to Anchorage and forfeited their deposit. It had to be that way to keep it clean. The one exception was if they had to leave because of sickness or death in their family.

They had a chapel and services on Sunday. Many people found Christ or recommitted their lives. They had the best guide service in the state with hunts for moose, bear, caribou, wolf, sheep. Hunts were ninety-nine percent successful, and moose hunters guaranteed a reasonable shot at a moose with a rack fifty inches wide or better. Dall sheep hunts were more because they required better-skilled guides who were in better shape physically, and the hunters also had to be in better shape, and a high outpost camp was also necessary. They were bringing in eighteen million a year but were only breaking even.

The lake was one of a kind. They have brought in kokanee, which are landlocked sockeye salmon. They grew to about five pounds. The lake was full of freshwater prawns. This accounted for their large size and proliferation. They would run up the river that fed into the lake and spawn and were able to replenish themselves. They had also planted them in all of the other area lakes on the property, and in the leased areas, the guests could take three fish a day for seven days. So many families came mostly just to fish, but most folks chose not to fish at all.

They were also supporting three orphanages, one in Nome, one in Tok, and one in Dillingham. All were for native or Eskimo children. This was their twelfth year here. They had done a lot.

The next year, Tony had planned to take a large crew and build trails into the lakes on the extended property and build lodges on each one. They had plans for four-wheel, snowmobile, and dogsled trips, where they would stay out two or three nights.

Back to Me and Mine

It was my fourteenth year in this wilderness wonderland. I have come to love it and enjoy every day spent in it. I had been remarkably healthy physically. I had now fully accepted that I would die here. After all, if I hadn't been rescued after all this time, it was not going to happen. I had asked myself often, why is it that God seems to always wait until the very last minute to act?

I had kept a diary and told of my time here—the ups and downs, the woes, the experiences and adventures, the close calls, the highs and lows of living. I had pinpointed the gold source and the stash and who it was to go to and be used for. There was so much more to be had. In effect, it was inexhaustible.

God is like that. His power, his knowing, his presence—all are inexhaustible. I didn't feel that anything I had found or done here was really mine. I now fully realized that God's hand had been upon me all the time. I had a cross to carry, but he had helped me, and I loved him for it and for what he had done in my spiritual life. It was, in effect, a total life changer. I was a steward for a season. Had I been faithful? My Father is rich in houses and lands; he holds the wealth of the world in his hands.

EXODUS

I was contemplating going to the valley and finishing my supper. I had put on a large rib eye of moose on the spit to roast over the open fire. I would cut off a steak and finish it on cast iron. I picked a couple of ears of corn to roast also. I had picked a peck of beans just because they needed picking. I would just cook them all and can what I didn't eat in the next couple of days.

I had made a really big cobbler of blueberries because they needed to be used up also. I peeled a couple of spuds and froze a gallon of ice cream. "You act like you're expecting company," I said to myself. It was early fall, a Friday in 1999. I will be sixty-two on my next birthday. I thought I heard a plane, then as I listened, it sounded more like a power saw, low down and to the south. That could only mean one thing: people!

I jumped on the quad, went over my floating bridge, and down my old trail to its end. I shut off the quad, and I could hear pounding and voices. I was beside myself with glee, the first voices I had heard besides my own for nearly fourteen years. I went through nearly two hundred feet of brush and small trees. I came to a small plateau where men were busy working. A fellow saw me and said, "You old sourdough, what are you doing here? Prospecting?"

I said, "No, I live here. I was just fixing to do supper when I heard your saws running."

"What's for supper?" he asked, chuckling.

"I'm having moose rib eye steak, fresh-baked bread, potatoes and gravy, fresh corn on the cob, green beans mixed in with ham and onions, blueberry cobbler with ice cream, and cold buttermilk to drink."

He just sort of laughed and said, "Sure you are."

A big broad-shouldered man with a shaved bald head came over and studied me for a moment and then asked, "Who are you?"

I said, "Well, I think I must be a man named Clint Terwilliger."

This man began to shake and cry and stumble toward me, saying, "Dad, Dad, Dad, I thought you were gone forever." He put me in a big bear hug, and we just stood there, shaking and crying.

It all came rushing back then. This was my son Tony. Everything cleared up. I mean, I really knew who I was, and I was going home. And after that, the men cut a fast trail through the brush to where I had left my quad. I led them back and up to the valley on the mountain. I seated them around my firepit with the roast slowly turning on the spit. My oven was hot from having a fire in it for the past three hours. The bricks were superhot, and I had four round loaves of bread ready to bake.

As I was shoving them into the oven, I heard screams and blasphemes and men scattering and diving for cover. Samson had followed us and now came running up to me. I put my arm around his neck and gave him a big pat then said, "You can come out now, men. It's only my teddy bear."

They reseated themselves and were trying to laugh it off. I said, "There's nothing to fear. There's some moose around too that are pets, so just calm down."

They all looked at each other like, "What is this guy anyway?"

Tony and I ran down to my field and got some more corn to roast and dug some more potatoes. I took them back and asked their cook to peel them and get them on to cook. I said I need to go down below and get the blueberry cobbler, the ice cream, butter, and buttermilk. He was all too happy to, and some of the men got their jackknives out to help.

I had a swing-in grill that I had made from a sheet of plate steel and swing-ins and hangers for kettles. I could cook a nice meal out here in the open. I preferred it. I only had silverware for six, but the cook had a set for each of these guys and round stainless plates and stainless cups. I took Tony down, and we went through the man cave, and I explained to him quickly and then on up to the big house.

You would have thought he was Alex in Wonderland. His mouth was hanging open with just awe then oh and wow coming out. I got the stuff I wanted, and we went back up. Later, we were ready to eat. I said, "Men, let's give thanks before we eat."

Those men all knew now how I got here and when. Some of them were Christians; some were not. As I began to pray and bless God for his power to keep and provide, God's Spirit settled upon us. Every one of those men wept openly, and three old sinner boys fell down and gave their hearts to Jesus.

We ate together, and the cook gave me a nice compliment. How could there be a gourmet cook way out here in this wilderness? Well, God has always been able to provide for those in the wilderness. I showed the men where they could all sleep in a real bed and the upper porch where they could see the falls, the eagles, and other birds and animals. I gave them each a bar of my special lye soap and showed them the pool where they could take a bath.

We all sat around the fire, and at their urging, I related how all this had come about: the crash and why I had survived, how I had come to find the cave and Samson, how God had provided my every need and how his hand had been upon me all the time. They sat spellbound. Tony gave them a week off.

I asked them not to kill my pets and where there was a nice fat young moose on the other side of the valley, where the gardens were, where the sheep grotto was, and how to get there. They could explore down below the lake, the plane, where to fish, and so forth. I had the door to my cave padlocked.

Tony and I left early on Saturday morning. I told him about Fort Knox and showed him where I had stashed the gold. He was awestruck. He related how he was just breaking even, and this was an answer to prayer—just at the right time, just at the last minute. He agreed it was really God's, and it should be used for God's work.

We got back to the lodge, and I cleaned up while Tony went to round up the family. I bathed and shaved and dressed in Tony's only suit. It was a white one. I felt a little awkward in it. Well, the family all came in, and they saw me, but not even my wife recognized me.

Tony pounded on the table and said, "My family! Meet your long lost daddy!"

There was crying and cheering and hugging and rejoicing. I began to rejoice also and cried out, "God, thank you for bringing me safely home and all this rejoicing and singing and this wonderful banquet and atmosphere."

God just spoke to my inner being. He said, *Son, you're not home yet, and you haven't heard rejoicing and singing yet, and this banquet is nothing compared to the marriage supper I have for my Son and his bride. Carry on, thou good and faithful servant.*

The end.

About the Author

Clinton (Clint) Terwilliger was raised on a Nebraska cattle ranch that was the homestead of his father. He was born in a sod house that was built in 1908. Because of his dad's bad health, he had to start working hard at an early age. This caused him to develop a strong work ethic that followed him through the rest of his life.

Clint's early life was somewhat lonely because of the remoteness of the homestead and having a slightly timid and reserved personality. Life centered on being on horseback nearly every day, whether it was breaking them to ride, working or moving cattle, checking and repairing fence lines, or riding to school.

In leisure times, Clint would ride to the river to fish, hunt, and trap. He always had a boyhood dream of moving to Alaska. He made many trips there to work, hunt, and fish in his adult life. Though he never did have a permanent residence in Alaska, this story is heavily influenced by the experiences, the encounters, and the adventures of the times spent there.